I0654405

DEFY HELL

NOXIOUS

ANATHEMA — *BOOK ONE*

YOLANDA OLSON
JENNIFER BENE

ISBN (e-book): 978-1-946722-68-3

ISBN (paperback): 978-1-946722-69-0

Cover design by Dez Purington, http://prettyininkcreations.com/

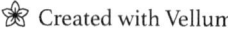 Created with Vellum

About Noxious

The Jackal

They say that the apple never really falls far from the tree—no matter how withered the branch or how rotten the core.

Don't get me wrong, I'm sure that my dad is a great guy, but he never counted on me showing up. None of them did, and that's exactly what's going to make this so fun.

We won't talk about my mother because chances are, he doesn't even remember who she is. To most people that's important, but not if you're a Meyer.

I just want to make amends with him before I move on—not that I've done him wrong, it's more the other way around. He was too busy getting his rocks off to be a father and that's understandable.

I don't fault him for it. Hell, I would have done the same thing.

Guess we'll see if he lives up to the legends I've heard about him because if I'm going this far, I expect fireworks.

The Tagalong

This better be worth my time.

I didn't want to drive hundreds of miles just to stare at someone that's supposed to be some kind of god.

But my partner-in-crime promises that whatever happens will be something neither of us will ever forget, and I never could say no to a good adventure.

I've heard weird rumors that his father lives with another man—someone he "won" from some girl they both used to hang out with, and honestly, that's the only reason I came.

Besides knowing that the jackal would lose what little grip he has left on reality if his father doesn't meet his expectations, I'm curious about how someone could be so easily manipulated.

Lucky for me, I'm not one of those people.

The Stowaway

If either of them find me, they're going to be pissed off.

I just hate that they're always going places without me when I want to go too. He told me that he was my friend but he slights me at every turn. She said she has nothing against me but she acts like I don't exist when he's around.

What's so special about him, anyway?

It can't be his personality because that sucks something fierce. He's the most arrogant person I've ever met in my life, but if I looked like him, I guess I would be as well.

He seemed really excited when they hopped in her car to drive to ... I don't even know where we're headed. I'm just lucky enough that they haven't found me yet and maybe when they do, they won't mind.

After all, where am I supposed to go when I'm in a place I won't even know?

ONE

Aces Wild

AFTYN

I roll the toothpick from one side of my mouth to the other, then lean back in my chair.

"Let's make a *real* bet for this hand," I challenge Willa, a smirk creeping across my lips.

She raises an eyebrow at me over her cards before she places them on the table and folds her hands over them.

"What do you think you have that I could possibly want?" she asks curiously.

I scoff and roll my eyes.

It's obvious she's just being a little bitch right now because I know she wants me. She has for a long while now, even if she won't admit it to herself.

I lower my eyes to the cards in my hands and bite down on the toothpick, the smirk on my face widening into a grin.

"Besides the obvious?" I retort as coolly as I can.

Reminding her that being a bitch actually turns me on won't help the situation any. "Anyway," I continue as I lean forward and place my elbows on the table. I shuffle the cards in my hands for a moment.

"The suspense is killing me, Aftyn," she remarks in a bored tone.

"I'm getting there," I snap. When Willa grins at me, I have to bite back the urge to toss the cards in her face, knock the table over, and fuck her until she begs me to stop. Not that I would—from what I understand, that's not the Meyer way and I'd love to live up to my old man's legend.

"So, if *I* win, then I get to fuck you," I say conversationally.

"And if I win?" she asks, rolling her eyes at me.

"Then you fuck me. Either way, it'll be a win for you and we both know it," I remind her smugly.

"How about if I win, you drop dead?" she barks at me as she picks up her cards, glaring at me over the top.

I let out a good-natured laugh. One of the very reasons I consider Willa my favorite frenemy is because of the cute little shit she says to me—like constantly telling me to drop dead.

"Would you fuck me if I died?" I ask her innocently, batting my eyes at her. Willa laughs and shakes her head. She can stand up for herself too, and in my book, that's a plus.

"Show me what you got, Wills," I say after I show her my hand.

All kings and a two of spades. There's no way this bitch will beat this hand. Not in a million—

"Fuck!" I shout angrily when she drops her four aces and three of hearts on my cards. I lean back in my chair and cross my arms over my chest, doing my best to control my temper.

It's not her fault that she always fucking wins, but I don't like losing. Especially not when there's pussy on the table.

"Back to the original bet, Meyer," she says as she tucks her legs underneath her on the chair. "Tell me why the hell you really want to go to Arizona and explain to me again why flying isn't an option."

I let out a loud sigh as I drop my hands into my lap before I run them back through my hair. I hate this heart-to-heart bullshit, but she seems to have a knack for it and Willa is one of the more curious creatures that I happen to be acquainted with.

With a shrug, I tell her for what seems like the one millionth time. "I found my old man's address. I think it would be kind of cool to see what he's like. Not to bond or anything stupid like that, but it would be nice to look him in the eyes just once."

"That's right," she says thoughtfully, "and why can't we fly?"

"I hear road trips can be fun. Besides, you've got

that fancy new car and you barely move the fucking thing. Wouldn't this be a great reason to break it in?"

She places an elbow on the table, drops her chin in her hand, and begins to drum her fingers along the tabletop. I know she hasn't made up her mind about this entire thing, and I know that me bringing it up almost every single day since I found the fucker's information online hasn't helped the situation any, but she'd be getting two of me for the price of one and that should be more than enough to say yes.

Okay, so I didn't exactly *find* him. I got a strange email one day from some random account that gave me the bare minimum when it comes to details and dared me to go to Arizona. I don't take dares very lightly and I don't back down from them either.

I sugarcoat that version of events for Willa because my acceptance of dares has gotten us into more trouble than most of them are worth. I believe in having a good time at any costs, she believes in common sense.

"I guess so," she finally says with a shrug. "We can leave tomorrow night if you want. I'll sleep all day and we can miss a lot of the bullshit traffic if we leave at an odd hour, anyway. Consider this your birthday present, Meyer," she finishes with a chuckle.

I grin and nod.

On the outside, I maintain my composure. On the inside, I'm freaking the fuck out. I've been trying for *weeks* to get Willa to fucking agree to this and all it took was a game of cards and some goddamn bantering about fucking her to get the job done. Had I known it would have been so easy, I would have done this the day I got the damn email.

I watch as Willa pushes her chair back and gets to her feet, rubbing her eyes tiredly. Glancing at the time on my phone, I suck my teeth before I turn my attention back to her. I didn't realize it was already half past midnight, but I guess the saying is true—time flies when you're having fun. Or scheming schemes; however it goes.

"Are you going to tell Dexter?" she asks, before covering her yawn with a closed fist.

I glare at her. "Why the fuck would I tell him about this?"

"Cause he wants your dick," she replies with a smirk. I clench my jaw almost instantly—I'm sick and tired of her pointing that out to me. A lot of people want my dick, but I'm not into guys and I've told him that a thousand times already.

"Just you and me on this one, kid," I say through gritted teeth. "And if you tell him about this, then one of us won't be making it back."

Willa shakes her head and rolls her eyes. She always thinks my threats are idle and never takes me seriously.

The problem with that is that I've felt an urge building inside of me as of late and she's been in the crosshairs of that feeling without even knowing it.

Great thoughts to rub one out to, if I do say so myself.

"I'll be back tomorrow night. Get some sleep because I'm not doing all of this goddamn driving alone."

Willa pats my head on the way past me and I cringe. She's going to learn one day soon that of the two of us, I'm the one in charge.

No matter how high up in the air she likes to stick her fucking nose around me.

Bitch.

TWO

Nocturnal Animals

WILLA

Aftyn is such a pain in the ass. He thinks he's the most amazing thing to grace the face of the Earth, but I always manage to hold my own against him.

Arrogant would be a good way to describe him, though I'm sure that's something he inherited more than learned. His momma never gave two shits about him—she always kept harping on him that he looked like 'that no good son of a bitch that left me as quickly as he found me.'

Aftyn likes to pretend that it doesn't bother him, but I'm not entirely sure that's true. Especially since he's threatened, begged, and then threatened me again to drive him to Arizona.

I yawn again, using the back of my hand to rub the tired feeling from my eyes.

I don't get why he can't give Dexter a damn chance either.

I know the thought irritates him to no end, but considering he's always trying to play grab ass with someone who doesn't want him—namely me—you'd think he throw a bone at someone that does.

In every sense of the word.

Of course, from what I understand, those Meyer men always want what they can't have and they don't give in so easily to the ones that worship the ground they walk on.

I wonder if his father is a dick too.

I roll my eyes at the thought as I stop at the red light. He has to be if his son is, cause he sure as fuck didn't get it from his momma.

He probably looks like a lot like him, I tell myself as the light finally turns green.

Aftyn is a tall guy—about six foot. Has messy, jet black hair, a pair of narrow, mischievous blue eyes that I swear hide the devil in them sometimes, and when he grins, it takes up half of his face.

I never do recall seeing his momma smile much. Not around him, anyway, but I do know he doesn't look a goddamn thing like her.

Or didn't, I correct myself with a chuckle. It's easy to forget sometimes that she died a few years ago only because we don't talk about it.

He didn't cry, if anything I don't think I've ever seen him happier than he was that day. Whatever was left inside of him that could be identified as moral shattered into teeny, tiny pieces and I picked them up as best as I could.

Lucky for him, when my granddaddy died, he left everything he ever owned to me since he wasn't on speaking terms with my father when he got sick. I used a lot of that to set up Aftyn comfortably in a fancy loft apartment over in Tribeca.

Sometimes, when the celebrities blow into town for that damn film festival, we'll sit in one of the windows of his place that looks down over the main road below and watch them mill around.

I grunt as I pull my SUV into the spot outside of my home. It's going to be over two thousand fucking miles just to get to the Arizona state line itself, and God knows how much further once we reach that.

Cracking my neck, I remove the keys from the ignition and grab my purse from the passenger seat. Once I've stepped out of my new ride, I press the alarm button and begin to search inside my purse as I head up my walkway.

Where the fuck are my house keys?

"You were gone for a long time."

I startle and swallow down a scream. I let out a relieved, yet annoyed, sigh when Dexter makes his way over from around the side of my house and slips his hands into his pockets.

In a way, I feel bad for the little fucker.

He's not short by any means, maybe an inch or two

shorter than Aftyn, but he's so damn gaunt looking these days that I wonder if he ever has enough to eat. Considering he lives in the same goddamn neighborhood that I do—a few doors down, no less—I would assume so.

Though something tells me that in order to keep up appearances for the *Stepfords*, as I call them, he cuts out necessities.

Like food.

"Come inside," I tell him tiredly after I finally retrieve the keys and slip them into the lock.

He scuffs his foot against the lawn, eyes on the ground, then nods when I reach over and give him a gentle tug.

Dexter is a really good-looking guy in his own 'needs saving from shit he doesn't know is bad for him' kind of a way. He's got hickory-brown hair that he always does his best to keep nice and neat. Sometimes I'm worried he's going to comb it all off, but I assume that he thinks if he looks presentable enough, maybe Aftyn will notice him the way he wants. His eyes are the color of rusty pennies, but it's my favorite thing about him. I've never seen eyes like his before and sometimes I lose myself staring into them.

It makes us both blush because I shouldn't be so damn easily captivated by a feature, but it's hard not to be.

"Were you... um," his voice trails off nervously as he walks in behind me and closes the door.

I smile at him over my shoulder. "Yeah. We were just playing cards though, honey."

His cheeks redden slightly, and he shrugs. "Oh, I don't really care. I just know that when you're gone for a long time, you're usually with him."

"Well, don't worry about it, Dex," I tell him, giving his arm a gentle squeeze. "That fucker has nothing I want so there's no competition from me, okay?"

He clears his throat and nods before he finally lifts his eyes from the floor and glances toward the kitchen.

"I think there's some leftover pot roast in the fridge," I say softly.

Dexter looks up at me with those hopeful eyes of his and I nod. That's all it takes for him to be off like a shot into the kitchen, rummaging around in the refrigerator before he finds the small container. I knew he'd come over to eat at some point, so I saved as much as I could for him. The rest went to Aftyn—not because he doesn't eat; he just doesn't know how to fucking cook, so I do that for him too.

Come to think of it, I think the only thing I don't do for him is wipe his goddamn ass.

Which reminds me.

"Hey, Dex?" I begin as I hop up onto the counter next to the stove. "I'm going out of town tomorrow night. Fuck knows how long I'll be gone, but before you leave, take the spare key, okay? It's in that tin jar on top of the fridge," I say, gesturing with my chin. "I gotta go get some sleep to get ready for the drive. I just want you to know that you can come and go as you please while I'm gone."

He clears his throat but doesn't say anything. He keeps his eyes trained on the microwave instead, his hands gripping the edge of the counter next to my legs, turning whiter than I've ever seen them and I sigh.

Hopping down, I lean over and give my friend a gentle kiss on the cheek, ruffle his hair for good measure, then call out a sound *good night* as I make my way back to my room.

As I lay down in my bed and pull my sheets up to my chin, I stare at the ceiling for a moment.

Something tells me that this is the last favor I'll ever do for Aftyn Meyer.

THREE

The Lateness of the Hour

DEXTER

Infomercials have always been my favorite thing to watch. I don't know why, but I'm assuming it's because of the overly cheerful way these people present their products.

Maybe they know that if anyone is watching at this hour it's because they can't sleep and shouting at them might help.

I clear my throat as I stare at the screen. Who the hell needs some kind of super scrub spray for their bathroom tiles? This guy seems really excited about it though, and the way he wipes the mold off after one spray and turns to look at the camera makes me chuckle quietly.

I look down at my small plate and use the fork to break off another piece of the pot roast, then pop it into my mouth.

Reheated leftovers never taste as good as the day before, but at least it's something. And honestly, there's only so much I can tighten my belt before I pass out from the hunger.

To say I can't afford to live in this neighborhood would be an understatement, but Willa has been the only person in my life that's ever been good to me and being close to her has always made me feel better about shit.

I met her the last year of high school.

We didn't go to the same one, since she's a year older than me. We were standing in line at the local Mom and Pop grocery shop and I was ten dollars short on the food I was trying to buy.

She reached over and swiped her credit card to make up the balance, then smiled at me and told me to have a nice day.

Her sleepy blue eyes got my attention first and foremost. They seemed full of secrets and dangerous things, but her million-watt smile froze me in place. Her long blonde hair has always looked like woven gold and I guess it reminds me of the girl that was locked in a tower by Rumpelstiltskin that spun straw into gold.

It made me wonder if there was any evil guarding the grounds of the proverbial castle, and that was confirmed the day I met Aftyn Meyer.

His mouth is my favorite thing about him. Not for

the rude and crude things that come from them when they part after a wicked smile, but because of how full they are.

My body shivers involuntary at the thought of him. He's never been nice to me, but he doesn't treat me like I don't belong either.

I think he likes having me around, especially when he's in a bad mood, because it gives him someone to unload his frustrations on.

The odd thing about this entire friendship, or lack thereof with those two, is that I'm not sure which of the two is the most beautiful and ergo, can't decide who I'd rather end up in bed with.

It's strange to me since I've never been attracted to a man before, but who the fuck could honestly look at Aftyn and not want to touch him? Even just a little bit?

Suddenly the day-old pot roast that I've been enjoying in the television-illuminated living room is starting to taste dry.

Thinking about him always makes me feel weird and I hate that I can't control the damn emotion.

With a sigh, I place the fork on the plate and lean back against the couch, turning my eyes toward the ceiling above me.

Willa said she was going on a road trip and she wouldn't be back for days. She said I was welcome to come and go as I please, but why do they always get to have the fun without me?

Just one time, I'd love to be able to fit in with them and be seen as an equal and not a hindrance. Not that she ever treats me like that, and I don't think he does it on purpose, but maybe if I can hang out with them for however long this takes without having anywhere to run off to, they'd see me in a different light.

Fuck it.

I get to my feet and pick up the plate. After I grab the remote and hit the power button, I walk into the kitchen and begin to wash the plate and fork, then place them in the strainer.

Once I'm done with that, I go to the refrigerator and grab the tin can that Willa pointed out, retrieve the key, then close my fist around it.

This way she'll think I'm staying home, I tell myself as confidently as I can, even though my body begins to tremble slightly. I feel crazy for what I'm about to do, and maybe even a little bold, but I want to know what's so great about them individually that they're almost always together without me.

I purse my lips as I begin to chew on the inside of my mouth nervously. Normally, I tell Willa when I'm leaving, even if she's asleep, because I don't want her to hear the front door opening and closing and think that someone broke in.

Not that it would ever scare her.

She's been into some really dark shit lately and I think it has to do with being Aftyn's friend.

I close my eyes for a moment and take a deep

breath, willing myself to be confident and to follow through with my plan.

Be brave, Dex. It's the only way to get things done.

I slip out of Willa's front door and close it quietly behind me, turning the knob to make sure it's locked before I run across her lawn, and the neighbor's after that, to get to my place.

I push the door open, which I never lock, because I figure if someone comes in and kills me, it would probably be a better thing than the way I live.

Not anymore, I tell myself as I head into my bedroom and quickly pack a bag. I make my way into the bathroom after I've put as many clean underwear, jeans, and shirts as I could fit into the duffle bag, then grab my toothbrush and toothpaste, assuming that there will be stops for showers and sleeping and I can slip out during those times.

Wait.

I go back into my room and lift the mattress, slide my hand under, and pull out the envelope full of cash. I don't trust banks, so I keep my money hidden in my home.

I don't count how much I have because I know that it should be just enough for this trip, and there are more stashes hidden here and there for the mortgage and utilities.

But not for food; never for food.

I shove the envelope to the bottom of the bag, then zip it up, and walk into my living room. I've never been one for sleeping. Insomnia is my best friend next to Willa, so I know I'll be able to stay up easily for as long as I need to in order to make sure I don't miss her leaving.

And when the opportunity presents itself, I'll figure out a way to go on their trip too.

FOUR

Alphas & Omegas

AFTYN

I took a shower about ten minutes ago and I've been laying on my bed naked, arms spread out to the sides, staring at the ceiling. I wonder if I really do look like him, if he even gives a fuck about knowing I exist, and how Willa's mouth would feel around my dick.

Oops.

I grin and chuckle at my last thought. Somehow, that little bitch gets to me in ways no one else has but she likes playing hard to get even though I'm sure she's finger fucked herself plenty of times thinking about me.

Focus.

I switch the thoughts of Willa off with a mental flick and go back to Lakyn. What kind of name is that, anyway? He's supposed to be this irresistible and brilliant maniac according to the email, but so am I.

Ever since I got the fucking thing, I've constantly

compared myself to the man that had a hand in my creation—the man I don't even know.

And in the quiet moments that I find myself thinking about him, the more I wonder why meeting him is a 'dare.'

Also, why now? Why not ten years ago when I was languishing under my mother's tyrannical iron rule?

That bitch never gave a shit about me. She hated me from the day I was born and treated me like garbage. I took it for as long as I could, though. Then, when the opportunity presented itself, I managed to get removed from her care.

It wasn't the last time I saw her though.

A smirk starts to cross my lips, but I decide that for now it's best to keep her and Lakyn as separate thoughts in my mind. I want to meet him first to see what the big deal is and if her hating me over him was worth the years she spent inadvertently making me into the man I've become today.

I turn on my side and bend a leg as I slip an arm under my pillow and glance at the clock. Three in the fucking morning and I'm still not tired enough to go to sleep.

I know Willa expects me to do some of the driving, but I want to do it all. If I'm going to be like Lakyn, I should probably act like him, and something tells me that he's one hell of a control freak.

He has to be.

How the hell else would he have lasted as long as he did if what the email said about him was true?

Not that there were too many details disclosed. Mostly just his name, a few addresses that he could be located at, a couple of pieces of information about the man, and the dare.

"I dare you."

As someone who likes to show people that I'm made of thick skin, something as simple as a dare will make me go above and beyond whatever the call of duty may be.

I roll my eyes and sigh when my cell phone vibrates on the nightstand next to the clock, then reach for it. If Willa is still awake, then I guess I'll be doing the fucking driving anyway, but I arch an eyebrow when I see I have a text message from a number I don't know and tap the screen twice to open it.

Chicken.

Rolling onto my back and assuming this is the same source of the phantom email, I run a hand over my face for a moment before I reply.

Who is this?

I let myself down expecting an immediate response, but I'm used to that. I let myself down a lot it seems with the expectations I set for every day, mundane things.

After ten minutes pass, I shrug and lay the phone on my bare chest then close my eyes, ready to try to get some sleep, when the phone vibrates again.

Are you going?

At this point, I'm over words. If this person won't tell me who they are, then there's only one way to respond. Opening the camera option on the phone, I tap the screen to turn the lens in my direction, hold up a middle finger and snap the picture.

I glance at it before I send it because even though stranger danger is a viable thing, this motherfucker needs to know that I'm as damn good looking as I am dangerous and I won't hesitate to fucking hurt them if given the chance.

I chuckle at my picture.

The sneer on my lips, the way my tongue sticks out of my mouth, and the way my finger is standing makes me look as mischievous as it does lackadaisical, both of which I feel toward the phantom that keeps egging me on.

I send the photo, then hold down the power button on my phone, placing it on the nightstand once it's off.

Time to get some shut eye, I tell myself as I turn back on my side again and do my best to drift off.

I grunt when I wake up the next morning. I'm pissed because I should still be asleep, but I guess it'll be up to Willa to take the night shift because no matter how hard I try, I just can't fucking sleep during the day.

I run my hands over my face a few times before I

smack my lips to get most of the taste of sleep out of my mouth, then glance over at the time.

It's almost noon which means I've slept for almost nine hours. I should be okay for driving later if she wants me to start the trip.

Swinging my legs over the side of the bed, I reach for my phone, power it on, then leave it on the nightstand as I head toward my bathroom to take a leak and brush my teeth.

I stretch my arms high over my head after I get back to my room a few moments later and smirk when I bring the screen to life.

Seems like my phantom replied after I shut the phone off and by the looks of it, it appears they sent a picture back.

I rub my eyes with one hand, stifle a yawn and click on the message.

That's when the air leaves my lungs and my legs start to tremble.

I sit down on the edge of the bed, and use my thumb and forefinger to widen the picture and stare in disbelief.

It's a picture of a man with black, tousled hair, narrow, blue, mischievous eyes, and a grin that I've seen staring back at me many times before in pictures of myself.

Almost like looking into a mirror, the accompanying message reads.

But without even having read that, I know that the man I'm looking at in the photo is Lakyn Meyer.

Maybe my mother's anger wasn't as misplaced as I thought it was because just seeing him makes me feel angry too.

I can't explain it.

Having such a sudden, undeniable hatred for a man I don't even know is overwhelming and as I toss my phone onto the bed, I wonder if this is exactly how he'll feel about me when I knock on his fucking door.

Game on, I think evenly as I take a deep breath, get back to my feet, and head over to the dresser. I pull out a fresh pair of briefs, jeans, and a loose-fitting t-shirt, getting dressed as quickly as I can before I walk over to my closet and begin to pack up for the trip.

And may be the best Meyer win.

FIVE

Old Gods, New Demons

WILLA

"Come on," I snap as I lay my hand on the horn for the third time. I don't know what's keeping Aftyn, but he had better not be asleep. It's almost nine-thirty at night and I want to get going.

As if to answer my question, the front door of his place opens and he tosses out a couple of bags, before he closes it again. If he thinks that I'm going to be his personal concierge, he's got another thing coming. Being his goddamn chauffeur is going to be bad enough because I'm not entirely sure that I trust him to drive.

He's not bad at it by any means, he just doesn't know what speed limits are. Or *any* limits at all for that matter.

I'm ready to lay on the horn again when his door opens, he steps out and almost trips over his bags. I rest my chin on the steering wheel and when our eyes meet, he gives me the finger before he picks them up and walks toward the vehicle.

Pushing open the driver's side door, I hop out and grin at him. "Sorry, but I'm not your maid."

"Noted," he replies with an eye roll as I pull open the door to the hatch and he tosses his bags in.

"What's got you in such a good mood already?" I ask curiously once he slams the hatch and turns to walk away.

Aftyn glances at me for a moment, eyeing me carefully before he blows out his breath and shakes his head. "Nothing. Let's get going before you change your mind."

The familiar curve of his lips makes me smile and shake my head. I know it's forced right now but he'll tell me what's wrong when he wants to and I won't press him.

That can have damning consequences as I've learned in the not so distant past.

"Hey, you're not gonna get all weird while we're doing this, are you?" he asks after I get back in the driver's seat.

"Weird how?" I inquire in confusion.

"You know..." his voice trails off as he straps his seatbelt on then turns to face me and holds up a forefinger and pinky on one hand.

I scowl at him as I turn the key in the ignition. Aftyn can never let anything go. I told him I once read about the Satanic cults in New Mexico after he told me about the email and how I wanted to stop just to take a look at their churches and stuff since we were passing through, and he's been convinced ever since that I worship the Devil.

It amazes me considering he's the only person in the world that deems himself worthy of such praise.

"I'll do my best not to sacrifice you," I snap at him as I glance into the side-view mirror, then pull out onto the street.

Universe and mythologies be damned; there's enough malice in the man sitting next to me that I don't have to invite anymore of it willingly into my life.

"So, are we there yet?" Aftyn asks as soon as we get stuck in gridlock traffic on the highway.

"We haven't even made it out of New York," I tell him with a glare.

"No wonder everything looks so familiar. Good idea, by the way. Leaving so late to dodge all of this. I guess construction hours slipped your mind, eh?"

I choose to ignore his snarky comments. I have to since it seems like Aftyn is already content on making this as miserable a trip for me as he can.

"This is the last time I do you a favor, Meyer," I grumble as I grip the steering wheel tightly in my hands.

He chuckles but doesn't say anything else.

This is just how we co-exist with each other, and even while sometimes we can get along without barbs and jabs, I like us best when we're like this. It keeps the rainbows and sunshine of our friendship sparkling.

"Hey, Willa?" he asks after another ten minutes of slowly creeping traffic.

"Yeah?"

"Can I show you something?"

"Sure. It's not like it'll put us in danger of crashing or anything," I reply with a shrug.

Aftyn shifts in his seat as he reaches into his pocket to retrieve his phone. I glance over at him when I see him staring it for a moment, the usual mischievous gleam in his eyes vacant, before he licks his lips and taps the screen to life.

"The emails have turned into text messages now," he begins slowly, "and when I turned on my phone this morning..."

At this point, I'm resting my elbow against the lower pane of the window, and eyes back on traffic when I feel him reach over and poke me.

"Sorry, I—"

To say that if I wasn't sitting in almost standstill traffic, I would have swerved from the shock would be an understatement. The man in the picture he's showing me looks almost exactly like him, except that his eyes are a little wider than I'm assuming Lakyn's.

"Crazy, huh?" he asks softly.

"That's a little more than crazy," I reply as I reach

over and take the phone from him, holding it closer so I can inspect the man.

This entire time, I thought that Aftyn was pulling my leg and just wanted to see how far he could push me in doing shit for him, but now that the evidence is in my hands, I kind of feel bad for judging him so quickly.

When I attempt to hand him the phone back, a grin starts to slip over his lips. I raise an eyebrow when he begins to undo his seatbelt, then shakes his head.

"Hold it for a little bit and keep your eyes on him. I wanna try something," he says in a thick voice as he leans over and places his chin on my shoulder.

"Aftyn, what—"

My breath hitches almost immediately when he slips a hand into the waistband of my jeans, pushes my panties aside, then roughly slides his fingers into my pussy.

I can't exactly say this is unlike him because what he wants, he goes after, but it's the first time he's ever put his hands on—or in me—like this before and I'm a little too scared and equally turned on to move.

"Don't close your eyes, cheater," he chuckles, his breath hot on my ear as he begins to move his fingers skillfully in and out of my wet opening.

My body begins to tremble as I stare at Lakyn Meyer's eyes while his son continues to drill me with his fingers.

"Which one of us do you like best?" he whispers into my ear as he moves his fingers faster.

When he moves his thumb to my clit and begins to rub it, while his fingers continue their assault, I do my best not to take my foot off the brake.

"Tell me," he grunts, as he slips his fingers in deeper.

And just as I open my mouth to make a sound other than labored breathing and shuddering gasps, the car behind us lays their hand on the horn. Aftyn lets out a frustrated groan as I use my shoulder to shove him away, toss his phone at him, and press gently on the gas.

"I almost had you," he says with an annoyed laugh.

I glance over at him and shake my head as my breathing begins to return to normal.

With a sigh, he tosses his phone into the backseat, opens the window on his side of the car, and retrieves a pack of smokes from the inside of his jacket pocket, lighting up, then turning his attention to the bright, flashing lights of the trucks blocking traffic in the middle and right lanes.

He's done now and until he feels like speaking again, this is going to be a longer ride than I thought.

Especially if he thinks I'm going to let him get away with doing what he just did without asking me first.

SIX

Breath Play

DEXTER

I waited until the car started moving to push Aftyn and Willa's bags off my head. It's not easy hiding in the back of her damn car, and while I'm uncomfortable, I know I have to do my best to stay quiet while they bicker and diddle each other.

The latter made me feel a little sick, though. I never knew those two were fucking each other. I had a feeling, I just thought she had more class than that, and that he had better taste.

Which is probably why neither of them ever want to be around me, I think miserably as I turn my head slightly. There's enough air under the heavy blanket she keeps in the back for me to keep breathing, but I'm pretty sure that I won't last much longer like this.

The incessant stop and go of traffic is making it worse. I never knew I was prone to car sickness until I put myself in this damn situation.

A sound *smack* greets my ears and I have to do my best not to laugh out loud. Maybe Willa has more class than I thought, but I'm pretty sure that isn't going to earn her any favors with Aftyn.

"If you *ever* do that again, I'll break your goddamn hand," he barks at her.

She giggles and in an even tone responds to his threat, "Likewise, Meyer."

"Are you serious?"

His tone is riddled with disbelief and contempt at her rejection of whatever the fuck he just did to her, but Willa doesn't back down.

"You already know that I don't like you that way. It's one thing when we're high or drunk, but sober? I don't want your grody hands on me."

"Bitch," he grumbles in defeat.

I shift slightly under the blanket as a grin settles over my face. While they seem to hate each other, I know they're the best of friends, and if I'm being honest, I like them best when they're barking at each other.

Aftyn's eyes become wide and dangerous when he gets angry, while Willa's take on a bored and superior look.

I wish I could see them now.

One of them lets out a sigh and the cool, night air comes breezing into the car followed immediately by the smell of tobacco.

"This is going to be much longer than it needs to be

if you're going to be a precious bitch about things," Aftyn tells her curtly.

"So what? You're a precious bitch about everything when you don't get what you want."

Silence.

Stony and harsh.

That's what follows next, then the sound of a car door opening, and footsteps walking away from the vehicle.

"Fucking crybaby," Willa mumbles as she pulls over on the side of the highway and the blinkers start to tick.

Another car door opens, closes, then footsteps running on the gravel.

An act of bravery descends on me as I push everything off my body, then sit up. Since the windows are tinted, I know they won't be able to see me right away and I'll have enough time to hide again before they do.

I push my hair out of my eyes as I sit up and press my nose against the window. They're not too far away from Willa's truck, and she seems to be trying to calm him down. He's looking down at her with that look he sometimes gets once something no longer holds his interest, and her hands are on his forearms while she talks. I can't hear a goddamn thing they're saying, but when one of the construction guys goes over and attempts to intervene, Aftyn takes one more drag from his smoke before he flicks it over the side of the highway.

With an eye roll, he shakes loose of Willa's hands and shoves his into his jacket pockets as he begins to walk back toward the truck.

I drop back so quickly that I hit my head on the side console and almost black out from the pain, but not before I manage to cover myself up for the most part.

I hear the car doors open then close again respectively along with Aftyn muttering his trademark, *whatever,* to Willa when she asks if he accepts her apology.

I close my eyes tightly and do my best not to vocalize the pain I'm feeling, but I fuck up. I shift again not paying attention to my surroundings and as the vehicle starts to creep up slowly, I accidentally hit one of the bags too hard and it makes a *thump* sound against the back seat.

"What the fuck was that?" Aftyn asks curiously.

"You heard it too?" Willa asks in an uncertain tone.

"Pull off when you get a chance. I'll give it a once over to make sure that nothing is fucked up," he tells her with another sigh.

Great, I think miserably as the darkness begins to descend over me. *Once he finds me, I bet they're going to leave me on the side of the road.*

SEVEN

Three To Win

AFTYN

"Alright, let's take a look," I say to myself as I hop out of the truck and begin to glance at the tires. Once I'm satisfied that those are still in top shape, I tell Willa to cut the engine. I know it's not above her to try and run me over, and I'm not taking any goddamn chances.

She hops out of the vehicle, then walks over to where I'm on my back. I glance at her for a moment, tilt my head to the side and grin.

"You know, if you weren't so high and mighty, I'd tell you to hop on right now."

"Get over yourself, Meyer," she replies with a laugh. I shrug as I shimmy under the truck. "Can you hand me my phone? I can't see a goddamn thing."

The door opens and closes again, "Here."

I reach a hand out blindly and grab it. "Thanks."

Tapping on the screen, I swipe the bottom menu down and hit the flashlight button. Everything underneath looks brand fucking new as far as I can tell.

I hold my phone out to her and after she takes it, I shimmy out from underneath and get to my feet, slapping the dust off the palms of my hands.

"Maybe you ran over something," I tell her with a shrug as she hands me my phone back.

"No way. I'm pretty sure that would have left a mark with as loud as it sounded."

I take a deep breath and remind myself to be patient. If she decides I'm being too much of a 'precious bitch' she'll go into Mommy-mode and turn the truck around, dropping me off at my front door, and I lose the dare by default.

"Okay, maybe you're right," I say as calmly as I can. "Pop the hatch and let's see what shook loose then."

With a nod, she leads the way toward the back of the truck and while I wait for her to open the door, my phone vibrates in my pocket.

Don't look. Not until you've had a chance to honestly calm down.

Once Willa opens the hatch door, I give her a gentle shove to the side and lean in. Nothing looks out of place, though and I can't quite put my finger on what the fucking noise was, but I know it happened because we both heard it.

I turn around and sit down, confused, a little pissed off, and ignoring the new round of buzzing coming from my pocket again.

Until...

"Get off!"

My face screws up in confusion as I look at Willa. She reaches for my jacket and pulls me out of the truck. I watch in confusion as she begins to toss our bags into the back seat, then whips back the heavy blanket she likes to have handy for whatever fucking reason, then I let out a loud sigh and turn my face up toward the night sky.

Unfuckingbelievable.

"Dexter!" she exclaims as she reaches in and helps him sit up. "Honey, are you okay? Your head is bleeding."

He winces at the tone of her voice then nods as he reaches back and rubs his head.

"New question, what are you doing here?" I intervene evenly.

"Can the god complex for now, Aftyn. I think he's really hurt," Willa says to me as she gets on her knees behind him and begins to move his hair to get a better look.

Like a fucking mother gorilla picking gnats off her baby.

"How sweet," I remark sarcastically.

Willa gives me a dangerous look over Dexter's hair and I smirk.

"Why don't you just say one of your fun little emo prayers over him. Think that might stop the bleeding?"

She scowls as she pulls her shirt over her head and

presses it against the back of his head. "We have to stop at urgent care; I think he needs stitches."

"Absolutely not," I shoot back, shaking my head. "We've got somewhere we need to be, so if he bleeds out, I'll be sure to pay for a power wash and some detailing."

"Ignore him," Willa instructs Dexter as she slides out of the truck, pulling him to his feet. He sways a few times before he's steady and smiles down at her. "Thanks."

"Get in the back and I'll swing by one of those twenty-four hour places. If Aftyn doesn't like it, he can walk the rest of the way."

"I'll be okay," he says quickly once he sees the look of outrage on my face. "If it doesn't stop bleeding, then I'll let you know, but for now, I guess you guys have somewhere you need to be."

I suck my teeth and decide to read my messages since I know that my mood is going to change anytime soon.

Think he'll love you?

I grit my teeth.

Whoever the fuck is doing this is going to have hell to pay because after I look my father in his fucking eyes, I'm going after this son of a bitch game player.

"Aftyn? Are you okay? You look a little crazy right now," Willa says cautiously.

"I'm fine," I bark.

Closing my eyes, I take a deep breath, hold it for

five seconds, the release it. *Let me try that again.* "I'm fine. Sorry about that. Are we ready?"

I do my best to wipe the sneer off my face, but I can tell by the look they exchange that I'm far from achieving it.

"We?" Dexter asks nervously, darting a glance at Willa.

I force a grin onto my face, "Fuck yeah. May as well come with us since we've gotten so far already."

I don't mean to sound as sarcastic as I do because I figure it'll make more sense to just let him come with us. Besides, if he was willing to almost die hiding in the back, he's probably a hell of a lot more fun than I've given him credit for.

Willa gives me a triumphant smile as she puts an arm around his shoulders, then turns and leads him toward the doors and I shake my head.

This was probably her fucking doing all along.

"So, can I ask you something?" I say to Dexter once she's pulled out of the empty parking lot. He meets my eyes in the side-view mirror and nods. "What exactly is your deal? I don't know you all that well, and we may as well start getting friendly since this is the hand we've been dealt."

He looks nervous and I smirk.

I love doing that to people.

Usually a question or a well-placed look and people shake in their goddamn shoes in front of me.

"Well?"

"Um, I'm not sure what you mean."

"He's my friend. He wants to be your friend too. The end," Willa intercedes as she pulls on to the highway.

I turn around in my seat, resting my chin on the side of my chair and look him right in the eyes. When he looks like he's about to piss himself out of fear, I reach over and rest a hand on his leg.

"To be continued."

EIGHT

Battleaxe pt. 1

WILLA

Aftyn fell asleep about ten minutes after asserting that his dick is bigger than all of ours.

He likes to be in charge, and even though he's far from it, I'll let him have this one. The last thing I needed was him making this trip longer than it needed to be because he was having one of his fucking tantrums.

I adjust the rear-view and smile when I see that Dex is asleep too. Of course, chances are he's more than likely unconscious, but that takes the work out of that for later.

I agreed to this stupid trip because not only do I want to be able to see if all of the Meyer men are insufferable assholes, but I know that if Aftyn's dad *does* live with another man, it'll give me an idea of how to handle these two.

I'd love for Dexter and Aftyn to hook up, but that seems like mission impossible for the time being.

I'll get some tips from his friend, I tell myself as I turn on the radio and lower it just enough to not wake either of my boys up.

I begin to hum along to the song that's on. It's one of those pop classics from the 80s that I honestly can't stand.

Anything to help myself stay awake at this point.

Aftyn shifts in his seat next to me and I half expect him to wake up, but he just crosses his arms over his chest and goes back to his soft snoring.

I turn my eyes back toward the road and shake my head, a smile on my face, and remember happier days, when he didn't even think of his father, and his mother was finally out of his fucking life.

"Be quiet," I tell him, giving the skin on his forearm a pinch. He hasn't stopped laughing like a goddamn animal ever since we've snuck in through the back door.

His mother has been entertaining her latest guest in the living room and Aftyn thinks it's hilarious to see her head bobbing up and down.

"What do you think they're up to?" he asks with a snicker. I glance at him and arch an eyebrow. For as long as I've known him, he's had a libido as high as the stars in the sky, so he knows exactly what they're doing right now.

"If you don't want us to get caught, we'll have to wait until she's done," I warn him as I take him by the hand and we creep back toward her bedroom.

He rolls his eyes but lets me lead the way. Once we're in her room, we crawl under her bed to wait for her guest to leave and for her to turn in for the night.

I never did like the way she treated Aftyn—she basically crucifies him every chance she gets for his father's sins and has never given him a chance to be himself.

At least, that's what he tells me, and since he's not allowed to have friends, I've never been over much when she's home. The one or two times that I have though, she's laid into him like he's the biggest pile of trash in the world and he just takes it.

Not anymore, I think grimly as he slides in beside me.

I turn my face toward him and when he glances at me, we both smile. Aftyn is my best friend in the whole world. Even though we honestly hate each other for the most part, we kind of know how to calm the other one down and it just works for us.

His full lips suddenly become a tight line of anger, and I reach over, take his free hand in mine, and give it a squeeze.

Seems that Mommy Dearest has gotten to the fucking portion of her 'entertainment special' and she sounds like a stuck pig squealing and moaning like a two-dollar whore.

"Hopefully it'll be over soon," I whisper to him as he turns his eyes toward the underbelly of the bed. His hand is shaking but I know it's not in fear; it's in anger, which he has every right to feel.

But not for much longer.

My Granddaddy died a few weeks ago and his estate lawyer already told me that I'm getting his gold mine. I promised Aftyn that I'd set him up with a new life. One far away from this bitch that makes his life a living hell, and I intend to follow through on it.

We just have to make sure she stays out of the fucking way of our plans.

An eternity, or thirty minutes later, the front door opens, then closes. She's finally gotten rid of Aftyn's latest 'uncle' and now the fun can begin. I always hated that she flaunts all of these bastards in his face, making him feel even less than zero, because she's so captivated by every man in the world except for her own son.

"Wills?"

I look at Aftyn whose eyes are wide and lower lip trembling. It's not because he's sad—he knew exactly what we were going to do tonight—I think it's because he can't believe that it's finally happening.

"Yeah?" I ask softly.

"Remember; me first."

His trembling lip gives way to a devious grin and I nod in agreement. He wants to make the first strike because he wants her to understand why, and I can honestly say that I admire him for that.

I cringe when I realize that his mother is going to bed without even showering. When her sweaty panties and skirt drop on the carpet, I reach over and turn Aftyn's face away. He shouldn't have to smell the stench of whore on her because I'm sure hearing it was enough to stoke the flames of rage inside of him as it is.

His breathing is normal which tells me that he's in control of his emotions. When he interlaces his fingers with mine, I know that he's ready. But when the confident look in his eyes is accompanied with that damn signature sneer of his, I know it's time to play.

Aftyn lets go of my hand as he slides out from one side and I from the other. His mother lets out a scream because she wasn't expecting us to be here, and when she begins to shout at him for being in her room, I reach forward, grab a fistful of her hair, and yank her back toward me.

Aftyn climbs onto the bed, knees on either side of her legs and leans down into her face, "Hi, Mom."

She begins to struggle violently against me when he places the small hatchet on the other side of his knee, but I tighten my grip and put the blade of mine against her throat.

"I'm not gonna be able to hold onto the bitch much longer," I bark at him as she reaches up and scratches the side of my face.

"Sorry, Wills. I just wanted her to look into the eyes she hates the most one last time," he tells me quietly before he picks up his hatchet again, raises it over his head, then brings it down as hard as he can, and when he hesitates for the slightest second, I tell him what he needs to hear.

"Do it, Aftyn. She deserves it."

NINE

Caught in the Middle

DEXTER

I've been feeling sick for the past hour or so, but I haven't spoken up yet. Partly because Aftyn is sound asleep, but mostly because I don't think he'd be too happy if we stopped again.

My eyes are slightly open as I watch the world outside go by in a blur. We finally made it out of New York about twenty minutes ago. I'm not sure what states are next, but I've never been outside of Scarsdale so this *should* be a great chance to see the world beyond the town's limits.

I reach up and gingerly touch the bump on the back of my head. It isn't wet anymore so I know it's stopped bleeding, which means I should be okay sooner rather than later. *One less thing for Aftyn to hate me over.*

"Hey."

I turn my head a little too quickly toward the front

of the truck, grimace, then smile at Willa's eyes in the rear-view mirror.

"Hey," I reply softly.

"How you doing back there?" she asks as she turns her eyes toward the highway again.

I shrug. "I'm okay, I guess. I'm not bleeding anymore."

She nods, then steals a glance at Aftyn who shifts in his chair, then goes back to snoring quietly.

"He could sleep through a goddamn nuclear war," she says with a chuckle.

I lean my head against the window again and go back to watching the blurry shadows of the landscape and occasional headlights of random cars breezing by us.

"Can I ask you something?" Willa finally says after a few moments of silence.

"Sure."

"How the hell did you get into the back of the car without me seeing you?"

I steal a glance at her eyes, smile nervously and wonder if I should tell her the truth. But when Aftyn shifts in his chair again, then sits up, I know the conversation is over.

"Where are we?" he asks in a groggy tone. I can hear the sound of him smacking his lips and it makes me smile. I don't want to fuck Aftyn—at least I don't think I do, but I wouldn't mind touching his mouth. To me, it's his best feature and deserves a little bit of praise.

"New Jersey."

"I guess that's better than nothing," he remarks as he sits up and leans forward. I close my eyes and listen to the sound of his bones popping as he stretches, then do my best not to open them again when I feel his eyes on me.

"He still asleep?" Aftyn asks Willa curiously.

"Yeah, but I'm pretty sure he's okay," she replies.

"Oh, I don't care about that," he tells her with a laugh. "I just wanna know if I'm paying for that power wash is all."

"Will there ever be a day where you care about anything other than yourself?" she barks at him.

"Hm."

I don't feel his eyes on me anymore, so I know he's turned around in his seat again, allowing me to crack an eye open without him knowing it.

"I don't see it happening if you want me to be honest, Wills. Someone has to give a shit about me, and we both know that no one will love me more than I do."

She chuckles despite the mood he's putting her in. I don't spend a lot of time with the two of them together, but for the most part, they seem to just snap at each other. This is different; he's trying to bait her, but she's refusing.

"Know what I was thinking about while you were asleep?" she asks thoughtfully.

"My dick?"

Willa lets out a loud sigh and Aftyn grins at her. "Never mind. You're clearly not in the mood to be an adult right now, and the sun will be up in a couple more hours. Go back to sleep so you can be ready to drive by then."

Aftyn turns his head quickly toward me and I'm praying that I closed my eyes in time for him not to notice I've been awake this entire time.

"I still can't believe he's here," he says.

"Why's that?"

"Because he doesn't belong on this trip, Wills. This was supposed to be ours to do alone and he weaseled his way in."

"No. He didn't. I invited him."

"What?" he barks at her.

I crack an eye open again and glance at Willa. I can see the smile on her lips in the rear-view and the mischief gleaming in her eyes. She's trying to save me from Aftyn unloading whatever seems to be bothering him, and she's willing to throw herself into his line of fire to make sure he doesn't do me harm.

But what's the worst that can happen?

I've seen Aftyn angry. His rage is unmatched by anything else I've ever seen, though I don't know him to be violent.

I can take a verbal lashing; hell, I'm used to it by now.

"I already told you what I suspect, Meyer," she tells him slowly, "and I didn't want to come back to him being starved to death because I wasn't around to open the goddamn door."

"Chicks," he snarls.

Willa laughs and Aftyn reclines his chair so that it's against my knees. Almost like he wants to make sure I can't get away from him, but where exactly can I go?

I'm at the mercy of the two people that know how to love and hate more than anyone else on this planet and I'm caught in the middle of whatever wave comes crashing next in the raging waters of their turmoil.

TEN

Legends and the People that Make Them

AFTYN

Once we've spent about three hours trying to get out of Pennsylvania, I've decided that I've had enough of sitting shotgun for a while. I refused to take over when Wills asked me to because I needed the extra time to think about things and I know that I couldn't do that if I had to concentrate on the road. However, I think now is as good a time as any to finally swap out.

"Pull over at the next rest stop," I tell her as I sit up and run a hand back through my hair. The incessant feeling of my phone vibrating in my pocket has been driving me fucking nuts and I know I can use that rage to put the pedal to the metal and cut some fucking time off this already too long drive.

Twenty minutes later, we're in a rest area with a couple of mom and pop cars parked and empty. I glance at Willa when she cuts the engine, then pull off my seat belt and turn to look at Dexter. He looks gaunt, a little pale, and sweatier than someone should be from just being in a goddamn car.

"You come with me," I say to him before I turn to look at Willa again. "We'll be back in little bit."

"Aftyn—"

"Chill out," I cut her off with an eye roll. "I promise not to hurt him."

Before she can shoot anything else out of her pie-hole, I hop out and stretch my arms over my head. When I turn around, I expect to see Dexter outside of the truck too, but he isn't.

I smirk as I press my nose against the window, then splay the palms of my hands on either side of my face.

He had his chance to come out the nice way, now I think I'll play a little game to see if he has enough balls to step out or if I have to drag him out.

I chuckle when I can see how rigid he is inside. Willa leans over and smacks the window to get me to move, but I don't turn my eyes away from Dexter.

I curve one of my fingers and tap at the pane of thick glass. He steals a look in my direction, but quickly turns his face forward again when our eyes meet.

"Come out and play with me, Dex," I say through the window.

Apparently Willa has had enough of my bullshit, because she uses one of the buttons on her console to lower the window causing me to grunt when the unexpected movement burns the skin on my nose.

I recover quickly because I know she wants to shit all over my mood right now and I refuse to give her that little victory.

I lean into the truck, resting my arms on the windowpane before I reach in and tuck Dexter's hair behind his ears.

"I'll let you blow me," I tell him.

When he turns his eyes toward me again, I bite my lower lip seductively. Granted, I'm not into guys, but a blow job is a blow job regardless of who it comes from and Ms. Frigid in the driver's seat obviously isn't feeling frisky these days.

"Um..."

His voice trails off as he darts his eyes toward Wills for help, but I look at her too and she can see the rage building if she tries to interfere right now. She wanted me to play nice? Then she's going to have to learn to play by my fucking rules.

"You don't have to get out of the car, Dexter," she tells him, glaring at me defiantly.

"You know what? She's right," I tell him as I reach into my front jacket pocket for my pack of smokes. Once I've got one firmly between my teeth and lit, I reach past him and grab the shirt she gave him to help stop the bleeding. I take a few steps to the left and open the gas tank, shoving the fucking rag inside. "You can stay inside and I can blow us all to hell, *or* you can get out and follow me into the bathroom. Your choice."

"Are you fucking crazy?" Willa shouts as she

frantically pushes open the driver's side door and leaps out of the truck. When she makes her way around to where I'm standing, I hold up a warning finger, my nostrils flaring, and she knows that she doesn't have a chance to stand against me right now.

I'm not in the mood for anymore kiddie bullshit. I'm ready to fucking play and get my goddamn rocks off.

"Get back in the truck, princess," I warn her through grit teeth. "Otherwise you're going to see a side of me that you won't be able to fucking handle."

"It's okay," Dexter finally says. I turn in time to see his door opening, followed by him stepping out. He walks over to the shirt and pulls it carefully out of the tank. "I'll toss this," he tells Willa as he begins to move his mopey ass up the walkway.

"Don't be jealous. If he's not good at this, you get to finish what he's about to start," I tell her with a smirk as I take a drag off my smoke.

"Why are you acting like this all of a sudden? This isn't like you at all," she says in disbelief.

I drop my cigarette to the gravel and crush it with my sneaker. "Don't pretend that you know me, Willa. You don't—no one fucking does. Get your ass in the passenger seat, I'll pick up the driving when we get back."

Before she has a chance to say anything else, I run a hand back through my hair, then shove them into my pockets as I take the same path that Dexter just took. I fish my vibrating phone out of my pocket and tap on the new text message that's been waiting calmly for the past few hours, read it, then scoff and put my phone away.

If anyone is in the bathroom, they're going to get a free show, and if they try to object.

Well...

Then I guess it'll be a chance for me to see just how much of bastard I can *really* be.

ELEVEN

Culling the Devil

THE AGITATOR

Ever since this began, I've wondered if it was the right thing to do. Another life will be ruined at the behest of Lakyn Meyer—but as he says, he's something that should be experienced at least once.

I guess it's not so much that I want to ruin the life of a young kid, but rather throw something at Lakyn that he can't fuck or kill his way out of.

There's a part of him that's human—no matter how hard he tries not to be—I know it has to be there.

I do my best to avoid him at all costs, though sometimes he crosses my thoughts in more ways than one, and I find myself wondering if he's been coping with life okay.

Not that he would ever admit to anything and sure as fuck wouldn't take too kindly to anyone asking, but...

I glance out of the window in the kitchen.

It's a nice day out so I think I'll go for a walk today just to be sure that our soon-to-be-mutual friend is still on his way.

If this doesn't go as planned, then I'll hear about it somehow. If it does, then maybe Lakyn will put his bullshit ways behind him and settle down with something for once.

Doubtful, I tell myself, a smile creeping across my lips.

If it doesn't revolve around Lakyn Meyer, chances are he won't give two fucks about it.

But this is different.

This is his child; he has to care about something like that, doesn't he?

Or maybe it's not his child and I got my information mixed up somehow, though I doubt that.

There isn't a secret in this world that Lakyn can't hide if he doesn't want to, and I wouldn't be surprised if more of them are walking around upright on two legs somewhere out in the cold, cruel world.

But I don't think this was a planned thing.

Someone must have gotten away from Lakyn—it's the only thing that would explain... um, Aftyn?

Fuck, I can't believe that I forgot his name already.

The sad truth about this is that I don't know who's going to be more disappointed if my little plan ever comes to fruition.

Me for having served someone up to Lakyn on a platter.

The latter for realizing that he isn't so perfect after all and managed to fuck up once.

Or the young man that I'm praying is on his way to look the devil in the eye.

Either way, I'll make sure that I'm nowhere near the radius blast when this bomb explodes.

With a sigh, I walk toward the living room, grab my jacket out of the closet and shrug it on.

"I'll be back later!" I call back over my shoulder as I hurry out the front door.

'I'm doing the right thing,' I tell myself confidently. *'It's not like I know how to do anything else. '*

TWELVE

Dexter, Undone

AFTYN

I'm leaning against the dirty bathroom sink, eyes on Willa's pet, and thoughts of what to do with him dancing in my head.

The easy thing to do would be to let him blow me, call it a day, then keep going, but I really never did like him.

It's nothing personal and never has been—I just see him as competition for Willa's attention and that's not something I want to have to fight for.

With as much bitching and moaning as she does about me keeping my hands to myself, I know she wants me.

I put a new smoke between my lips and light it, inhaling deeply before I use the tip of my thumb to rub the center of my forehead.

Think, Aftyn.

"Can I ask you something?" Dexter asks nervously.

"If you must," I reply with a grin. I flick the ashes off the end of my smoke before I place it between my lips and take another drag. Willa hates when her SUV smells like cigarettes, but she sure didn't seem to mind when the scent of her pussy caught in the air after a quick finger-fuck.

Focus.

"You don't like me, do you?" he finally says.

"Nope."

"Why?"

"Don't like people that can't stand up for themselves. You've had an easier life than most and you're too busy wanting Willa and I to notice you that you've shit all over everything you had and have to eat from the scraps of her table. What's to like about someone like that?"

He looks like I've slapped him in the face, and to be quite honest, sometimes a little spank here and there is required to make someone pay attention.

And I do like my spankings.

"Then why did you let me come on this trip?" he presses in his miserable confusion.

"Let you?" I ask with a good-natured laugh. "Kid, you hid in the back of the fucking truck."

He scuffs the tip of his sneaker against the grody bathroom floor and I grimace. Yeah, I need to get the fuck out of here and quick.

"So, my turn to ask you something," I say as casually as I can.

Dexter raises his eyes to mine and it takes everything in my power not to flick the ashes from my smoke into his face. For someone that wants so desperately to be part of 'the crowd' he sure does buckle under the weight of rejection rather quickly.

"Yeah?" he asks in a melancholy tone.

I take another drag from my smoke before I grip it between my teeth then reach for the zipper in my jeans. I keep my eyes on him as I pull it down and slip a hand in to grab my dick and get myself hard.

His skin turns a pale shade of white and I chuckle as I remove the smoke from my lips and continue to rub my dick where he can't see it happening.

Teasing is an art and I'm a fucking Picasso when it comes to it if I do say so myself.

"Aftyn?" he presses, his voice cracking slightly. But his eyes? They never leave where they're firmly planted watching me and hoping for just a peak or maybe even a little taste.

"Hm?" I ask, my breath hitching slightly. *I better stop before I come.* But I don't. I continue to rub my cock because it feels damn amazing—especially when someone is as good at it as I am.

Focus, I tell myself again as I take another drag from my smoke.

I cut my eyes toward the doorway when a man walks in and stops cold when he sees me playing exhibitionist.

"Sorry," he stammers as he turns and makes a hasty escape.

Pussy, I think with a smirk.

"See that?" I ask Dexter in a thick voice. "That is you in about twenty years. You see something that scares you and you run away instead of taking what you want."

The look of misery in his eyes spills over onto his face before it's replaced by bravery. I watch and wait as he squares his shoulders and then takes the few steps between us, closing the gap until he's so goddamn close that I can smell the sweat on him.

"Well?" I press him as I pull my hand out of my jeans and grip the bathroom sink behind me. "Do you want to be like him, or do you want to be someone with a backbone?"

Taking a deep breath, he reaches a hand forward and I wait.

Seconds can feel like years in situations like this, but patience is a virtue.

The moment he begins to slide a hand into my jeans, is when I remember that I was never a very patient guy.

It takes less time for me to wrap an arm around his throat and shift him so that his back is now pressed against my front and as he begins to struggle, I take another drag from my smoke.

"Maybe next time you should wish on a star that isn't already dead," I whisper hotly into his ear.

As Dexter continues to struggle against me, I toss my smoke onto the floor and reach around to grip my wrist and apply pressure. It'll take some time for him to pass out, then the oxygen will stop going to that pathetic brain of his that thought this was a possibility. After that, he won't be my problem anymore.

Or anyone's for that matter.

As he continues his futile little fight, I grin.

Maybe I'm more patient than I thought.

Once I made sure the little prick was dead and out of my hair, I stuffed him into the last stall in the bathroom. I used his body to jam the goddamn thing closed so I know that no one will find him until he starts to rot and by then, no one will ever be able to find me anyway.

I walk over to the sink and scoop up my discarded smoke, flush it down the toilet closest to me, then wash my hands.

Willa is gonna have a fucking fit, but I'll handle that however I need to.

Once I've dried my hands, I grin at my reflection, run a hand back through my hair and exit the building.

I can see Wills standing impatiently against her SUV in the not-so-far distance and I roll my eyes.

Clearing my throat, I begin to walk down the path

leading to where she's waiting when I see something out of the corner of the eye that catches my attention.

Something beautiful.

Something innocent.

Something that looks a little lost.

"Hey!" I call out, the grin returning to my face.

The beautiful, innocent, lost thing turns to glance at me over its shoulder and the grin on my face widens.

Maybe now is the time for Willa to find out what competition for attention feels like.

I walk over and sit down on the edge of the sidewalk next to her and offer her a smoke which she declines with a smile on her face.

This goddamn trip is finally about to get fun.

THIRTEEN

Sugar and Spice and Not Very Nice

DAPHNE

"Hey!"

Ding, ding, ding. We have a winner.

There's just nothing quite like sitting on a curb at a rest stop to bait the next wannabe gentleman to come to my rescue, but normally they're a lot older and a lot less attractive than the one who drops onto the edge of the sidewalk beside me.

He offers me a pack of cigarettes, and I glance at him for a second, shaking my head with a bit of a smile. Demure, face angled down, eyes up. Just long enough to get a look at him, and let him take one too, then I turn back to the parking lot, wrapping my arm tighter around my backpack.

"You need a ride?" he asks, popping a cigarette between his teeth and lighting it up. The cloud of smoke he releases taints the smell of fresh trees around us, but I'll allow it since he might be my ticket out of this parking lot. Still, there's something to be said for playing hard to get.

"Um..." I peek at him quickly before hitching my shoulders up. Defensive posture, nervous little girl... it's like ringing a goddamn dinner bell. Even if this guy falls through, there's another in a red shirt hovering around the back end of his Honda Civic that's been trying to build up the balls to talk to me for at least ten minutes. "I— Maybe?"

The guy laughs and blows out another stream of smoke, his blue eyes sparkling with something more than just the same old boring attraction. "Come on. You're coming with us."

Us?

"Where are you headed?" I ask, and he smirks at me like he thinks the question is cute.

"Away from here." He hooks his arm through mine and lifts me off the ground easily, but I have my backpack in my other hand, and that's all I really need as he half-drags me down the path. I look around for the skinny guy he went to the bathroom with, but I don't seem him anywhere. Instead, it looks like we're heading to a shiny new SUV where an irritated looking blonde is waiting for him.

Ah, us.

Tall, dark, and handsome has a pretty little girlfriend. Great.

"What the fuck, Aftyn!" she screeches, and he opens the backdoor for me with a grin, tilting his head toward it as the girl behind him fumes. "Aftyn! Who the hell is this? Where's Dexter?"

Biting down on my urge to smile at the chaos he's brewing, I climb into the backseat and buckle in, tucking my backpack into my lap. Aftyn slams the door and then struts around the front, dropping the cigarette beside the driver's door before he hops in. The blonde is still standing outside the car when he buckles his seatbelt and turns the car on.

The passenger window slowly slides down and he leans across the seats. "Willa, get in the goddamn car."

"Fuck off, Aftyn. Where's Dexter?"

"He decided to find a new beau in the bathroom," Aftyn answers with a laugh that dies a little too fast. "Last chance to get your ass in the car before I leave."

"We're not leaving without Dex. Stop being such an asshole."

"Okay, then." Aftyn shifts the SUV into drive and pulls forward a few feet, breaking hard when the girl screeches again, catching up to slam her hand on the door.

"What the hell are you doing?"

Sighing heavily, he looks over at her and pats the passenger seat. "I already told you that was your last chance, Willa, but I'm graciously giving you one more. Get in the fucking car or I'm leaving you here."

The pretty blonde looks like she might be about to cry, but she clenches her jaw and opens the door to climb in. Her ass is barely in the seat when Aftyn floors it, slamming the door shut from the force. She's fuming as she yanks on her seatbelt a few times before it finally gives and lets her buckle.

"Oh, Wills. I'm so glad you decided to join us. It just wouldn't have been the same without you," Aftyn says, and his voice is like a knife through silk.

"Tell me where Dex is. Right now." She's feisty, and I'm enjoying the little show from the backseat when those blue eyes suddenly look at me in the rear-view and I school my expression into wide-eyed interest.

"You're being rude, Wills. We have a guest. Her name is—" Aftyn glances at me in the mirror again.

"Daphne," I fill in, and he laughs.

"*Daphne.* She's cute, don't you think?" He seems to be enjoying himself greatly as the SUV picks up speed, weaving in and out of the slower moving cars on the highway without a single click of a blinker.

"I swear, Aftyn. If you hurt Dexter, I—"

"You'll *what*?" he asks, taking his eyes off the road to stare right at the blonde, and the smirk on his full lips seems like it was meant for his face.

"Pay attention to the fucking road!" she shouts, but he doesn't look away from her.

"I want to hear what you'll do to me. Want to tie me up and punish me? Treat me like a naughty boy?" Aftyn clicks his teeth together in a mock bite. "I might like that."

The blonde bites down on her lower lip, looking between him and the road ahead, and when she finally speaks again her voice is a lot calmer. "I just want to know what you did to Dexter."

"I don't want to talk about him anymore. It's boring," Aftyn replies, waving a hand at her as he faces the road and swerves around a car ahead, speeding up again as he glances at me in the rear-view. "Daphne, why is a pretty little thing like you out hitchhiking?"

"Just trying to get to some family out West," I answer, keeping my voice quiet as I pick one of the lies out of my hat of bullshit. "I appreciate you offering me a ride."

"Yeah, well, don't expect it to last long," the blonde bitch says, and Aftyn laughs again.

"Damn, Wills, look at you! Showing your claws already. What did she do to piss you off?"

"Apparently she took Dex's space in the backseat just because you liked the way she looked." Willa glares at me in the side-view mirror, a haughty sneer twisting her lips. "And she doesn't seem like much to look at."

"I don't know, she's got a certain innocence about her that I don't think you've had since you were a toddler." Aftyn grins, and Willa huffs, sinking down in the passenger seat as she starts tapping away on her cellphone. "What do you say, Daphne? Up for a road trip?"

"Sounds fun," I smile back at him in the mirror, and he holds my gaze for longer this time. I'm not sure what it is about him, but I'm intrigued.

"Damn straight it sounds fun!" he shouts, rolling down the window to shout into the whipping wind, and I laugh at his antics, mostly just to piss off the bitch in the passenger seat that's doing nothing but scowling at both of us.

I'm not sure who Aftyn is, but he isn't some asshole with white knight syndrome looking to rescue the damsel. If anything, he looks a lot more like the wolf stalking little red in the forest. Unfortunately for him, I've never minded cutting my way out of a wolf when they get too close.

If he tries something, he'll learn that I'm sugar and spice and not very nice, and I'll happily leave him and his girlfriend in a ditch and drive their shiny SUV until it runs out of gas.

Vroom vroom. Road trip time.

FOURTEEN

Rest Area Leftovers

WILLA

I don't trust the girl in the backseat. Not just because she's the reason that Dexter is gone now, but because she caught Aftyn's attention somehow.

Normally that's easy enough to do. All it takes is his goddamn hormones going into overdrive when he sees something that's prettier than he is, though I don't think that was the case here.

Aftyn has always been calculated and crafty when he picks who he hangs around with, and this new girl is no exception.

Did she say the right thing? Does he see potential in her? *Am I next?*

"Stop being such a spoil sport," Aftyn tells me softly as he reaches over and gives my shoulder a squeeze. "This was supposed to be a two-person trip to begin with, Wills. Dexter decided he wanted to go home, so I gave him some cash and left him in the restroom. He'll be fine," he assures me as he removes his hand and reaches for the pack of cigarettes he placed inside the visor.

"You promise?" I ask him quietly.

He clears his throat as he lights up another smoke and takes a deep drag. When he glances at me, I watch the smoke billow from the corner of his mouth, before his lips turn up into that damn dangerous grin he's so fond of giving me.

"Scout's honor."

"It's about fucking time."

I sit up with a start and let out a groan. I had fallen asleep with Aftyn driving somehow, but apparently, my neck decided to play the old stiffening game while I was out.

Rubbing my eyes tiredly, I blink a few times before they focus on what Aftyn was babbling about.

Ohio Welcomes You to the Heart of it All!

Hokey, but I like it.

For some reason it makes me feel safe in a vehicle where that no longer seems to be an option.

"Want me to take over for a bit?" I ask him in a froggy tone. Aftyn grins at me and I clear my throat, then try again. "Are you still okay to drive, or do you want to hand over the reins?"

"I'm okay," he replies with a shrug. "You did a lot of

the first part, so I don't mind getting us through and out of Ohio."

The delicate sound of someone covering a cough from the back of my SUV greets my ears and I lean around the seat to smile, when I'm met with a stark reminder that Dexter is no longer with us, but rather some red-haired, pretty little bitch that's probably here to take my place.

My mouth tightens into a line as Daphne and I stare at each other before I turn back around and reach down for my purse that's settled between my feet. I pull it up into my lap and begin to fish around until I find the small, clear bottle of hand sanitizer, then toss it over my head and hide a smirk when I hear the dull *thunk* of it cracking her in the skull.

"Thanks," she replies cheerfully as the top flicks open and I cringe. I don't want her to thank me, I want her to fight back so I can show Aftyn who the alpha is here.

Because it's definitely not you or her, I think as I steal a glance at him through narrowed eyes.

Aftyn seems to have slipped into his oblivious mode. I don't mind it sometimes, although it can take forever to get him to start paying attention to whatever is needed when he does.

It's his quiet moment time and I usually don't like to bother him when he's like this, however, he bothered me first by leaving Dexter behind and bringing this bitch in his place.

"So, Aftyn," I begin slowly.

"What's up, Wills?" he asks in a distracted tone as he suddenly accelerates and swerves around the car in front of us that he decided was going too slow. I brace myself by placing a hand on the console and digging into the interior roof with my other hand.

"Um..." *Fuck. I didn't expect him to actually answer me. Think, Willa. Keep him with you instead off in la-la land.* "Anymore text messages?"

"Wouldn't be able to tell you; I'm driving, remember?" he replies in an icy tone.

I lean back in my seat and sigh.

It seems that this is definitely a soft spot in his armor, though I know that after years of being Aftyn's friend, that nothing is ever as it seems.

Whatever is bothering him about going to see his father has nothing to do with anything he's told me, and it only makes me even more curious.

Although...

"Do you think that he's going to be impressed with a stranger in his house?" I ask pointedly.

If you can't play nice, then neither will I.

"How the fuck would I know, Wills? I don't exactly know the man," he replies testily. I steal another glance at Aftyn and bite back my smile when I see how tense his jaw is. He has a bad habit of grinding his teeth when he's in a mood and if he keeps it up, he won't have any left by the time we get to Arizona.

Taking a deep breath, I push the button of the

seatbelt and pull it off before I turn around in my seat. I get to my knees and place my chin on the top of the headrest and glare at the bitch in the backseat.

You're the reason that Dexter is gone, I think bitterly. *And I won't fucking forget it.*

FIFTEEN

Quiet Walks & Ticking Clocks

THE AGITATOR

Every now and then, I find time for myself. I'm able to go to the store to pick up some groceries or even just take a nice, long walk like I'm doing now.

Granted, it usually starts an argument, but that's okay. I know that not everything can be what everyone wants and that's why I started this little game of cat and mouse.

I got the idea one night when I was lying in bed struggling to fall asleep and staring at the ceiling. I was alone for the evening and it bothered me. Not so much the empty spot next to me, but the fact that I didn't have anyone to talk to.

I came up with a plan then, did a little research, and found exactly what I knew I would need to get by.

It started with an encrypted email.

Slowly, over the course of a few weeks, I began to

lay a trap for my soon to be new friend and painstakingly persisted until I finally got a response.

It's been a game since then.

But I haven't heard from him for the better part of a day and now I'm wondering if he's not everything I thought he might be.

I let out a heavy sigh as I bring my hand up to block the sun as best as I can. I don't even know what street I'm on, but I'm far enough away from home that I can sit down in the park across the street and try again.

After I've crossed the road, I make my way to the bench and sit down. I begin to chew the inside of my mouth thoughtfully.

Is this really worth fucking up this young kid's life? Seeing Lakyn Meyer face to face is something that ruins most people, but I guess I'm curious if he would even care or not.

Either of them, since I assume he's like his father.

I just have to make sure that I'm there when it happens, I remind myself with a chuckle.

I fish my phone out of my pocket and use the sleeve of my shirt to wipe the screen before I tap it to life.

He still hasn't replied.

I know I shouldn't feel as annoyed as I do but this isn't fair. I'm doing him a favor by helping him meet Lakyn and he seems to take more pleasure in dismissing the fact instead of being grateful.

Just like Lakyn, I think with an eye roll as I tap the messages tab and click on Aftyn's name.

Aftyn.

What kind of name is that, anyway?

Who the hell named these Meyer men?

With a shake of my head, I move my fingers quickly over the letters and then sit back to read my message. I hit the delete button a couple of times, retype some new words, then hit send when I'm satisfied.

Come on, Aftyn, I think as I close my eyes and cross my arms over my chest. *Don't let me down.*

SIXTEEN

Secrets in Empty Seats

DAPHNE

"I like your eyes," I say, smiling at Willa as she glares at me over the back of her seat. The flash of confusion on her face makes me want to laugh, or rip out those pretty blues with my bare fingers, but I swallow it down. Holding out the hand sanitizer, I tilt it back and forth. "Did you want this back?"

"Of course," she sneers, ripping it from my fingers to throw it into her purse. "I just wanted to make sure at least *part* of you was clean since you're in my car."

"It's a nice car."

Willa twists around in the seat again, rolling her pretty blue eyes at me. "Yes, it is, but I'm sure you want us to drop you off somewhere soon. How does the middle of fucking nowhere in Ohio sound?"

"No, thanks. I'll go as far West as you'll take me," I answer, holding onto the smile by digging my fingernails into my palm.

"How does Arizona sound?" Aftyn asks in a casual way, blowing another cloud of smoke out the window.

"That's perfect." I've never been that far west, but it does put me pretty close to California, and I could have so much fun out there. "Thanks again for the ride."

"She is *not* staying in this car all the way to Arizona! Not fucking happening." Willa turns to face Aftyn again, and I wonder how long they've been together.

"Why not?" Aftyn sounds almost bored, not rising to Willa's sniping tone.

"We don't know her! And you said you sent Dexter home because this trip was supposed to be just us." She waves a hand at me in the backseat. "This isn't just the two of us."

"Daphne, what's your favorite color?" Aftyn asks, looking at me in the rearview mirror, and I smile at him.

"Red?"

"Fantastic. See, Wills? Now we know something about Daphne."

"I don't *want* to know anything about the roadside prostitute you decided to pick up, Aftyn." Turning around in her seat again, she glares at me. "That's the only reason he picked you up. I won't fuck him, so he grabbed you because you're easy."

"Being easy would make me a slut, wouldn't it?" I ask, pretending to think over her pathetic attempt at an insult. "Prostitutes charge for everything, which sounds a lot more difficult. So, which are you going for, Willa? Am I a slut or a prostitute?"

"Oh shit!" Aftyn laughs loudly, banging a hand on the steering wheel before he takes a long drag on his cigarette. "Well, answer her, Wills. Slut or a whore?"

"Fuck off," Willa says, facing front again, and Aftyn grins at me in the rearview.

"Ignore her. Wills just didn't expect you to stand up to her." Aftyn reaches over toward Willa and she jumps, cursing at him as she shoves his hand away, but he just starts laughing again. "Go back to sleep. You're no fun when you're tired and bitchy."

"You're an asshole, Aftyn," Willa grumbles, huddling against the door again.

I'm not sure what's going on with these two. Neither of them seem particularly happy with the other, so maybe it's more habit than actual interest. Especially if she isn't fucking him anymore. I just don't know why she wouldn't be. He's hot, and he has a wicked tilt to his smile that tells me he could be a lot of fun.

Leaning against the window, I look at the small smear of dull red on the other side of the vehicle. It's on the plastic edge of the door, and I'm pretty sure it's blood.

I've spent the last couple of hours pretending to sleep while trying to figure out if these two are more dangerous than they appear. The previous occupant in the backseat, 'Dexter,' walked into the bathroom with Aftyn—but he didn't come back to the car.

Maybe Dexter hasn't been their only guest in the backseat though. The smear isn't enough blood for a murder scene... but it's definitely more than a papercut. Not proof of anything.

But it is interesting.

Dexter. Dexter. Dexter. Who were you?

Willa seems sincerely concerned about their old road trip partner, but Aftyn doesn't give a shit. If anything, he's shut down every conversation about the guy.

So many questions that I just can't ask.

Not yet.

Shifting, I slowly unzip the side of my backpack and reach in to brush the edge of one of my knives. It's a comfort thing, especially when I'm starting to get tired, but I won't sleep yet.

Not until I have a good idea of who exactly I've taken a ride from, and why there's blood in Willa's shiny new car.

SEVENTEEN

A Moment Suspended in Time

AFTYN

The sun went down an hour ago.

I've rubbed my eyes one too many times to pull over in this rest area and not get out and stretch my legs.

Willa is asleep again and even that Daphne girl seemed to be knocked out by the time I pulled in.

I'm leaning against the fender of Willa's SUV, a cigarette dangling from my lips. My hands are on my knees and my eyes are closed. I'm trying to convince myself that this is the right thing to do. That going to meet a man that had a hand in my making, but never seemed to give enough of a shit to even send a birthday card, is absolutely worth all of the trouble and may be worth even more.

I crack my neck when I open my eyes again and stand up straight. Thinking of Lakyn reminds me I've got unread messages on my phone that I've been forced to avoid due to driving for so damn long.

I fish the phone out of my pocket and let another billow of smoke escape my lips as I weigh my current options. I can either see what's waiting for me, or I can just shut the fucking thing off until we get to our destination.

Raising my eyes, I glance to my left when another car pulls in. It's a young couple; a man and a woman, and when they exit their vehicle, I chuckle slightly. *He looks a lot like Dexter,* I think as they walk by me.

I nod at him when our eyes meet, and he returns the gesture as he wraps an arm protectively around his gal.

If only he knew that I had two of my own right now, he'd probably feel a little more at ease since I'm not interested in his pussy.

Not that she wouldn't make a great addition to my little cult. She's got long, thick caramel-colored hair, a thick ass, and a pair of small, but perky tits.

I just don't have the room for her right now, and I'm pretty content with what I have, so I give him a two-fingered salute and watch them until they disappear into the restroom building.

I decide that its best to go back to my current predicament though and tap the phone screen to life. *Three unread messages? Someone is feeling a little desperate.*

The messages are all different, but I can feel the urgency in them as I read them back to back. The first one is asking if I'm on course to Arizona and if I'm excited to meet Lakyn. The second is asking how much longer I think it will take and requesting a current location, while the third is asking me if I'm still alive or if I've chickened out.

I clear my throat as I place my smoke between my lips again and begin to fire off a series of my own messages.

Currently somewhere in bumfuck, Ohio.

I have no idea how long this will take; sometimes a guy needs to stop for a bite to eat, to take a leak, or deal with the pussy in his ride.

Guess we'll see who's chicken here soon, motherfucker.

I press the button on the side of my phone to turn the screen off and just as I'm about to tuck it back into my pocket, the fucking thing vibrates.

I push away from the fender and crack my neck from side to side as I part my lips and let the cigarette fall to the pavement. I snuff it out with my sneaker before I wander over toward the small picnic area and take a seat at one of the benches.

I run a hand over my face before I tap the screen back to life and see the small envelope waiting for me.

One message.

A new one.

Sent almost immediately.

But I'm sick of phantoms hiding in the dark trying to dictate my little adventure here, so I swipe away the notification, open the message, and hit the call button.

The phone rings for an extremely annoying number of seconds that turn into minutes, but I'm a hell of a lot more patient than Willa ever gives me credit for.

Instead of giving up, I press the speaker button and toss my phone onto the bench next to me as I lean forward and rub my face again. I need to wake up more so I can keep driving. I told Wills that once we were out of Ohio it was her turn to drive again, and I don't want to make any more unnecessary stops along the way.

When the line clicks, I reach for the phone so quickly that I drop it against the ground.

"Fuck," I grumble as I scramble to pick it up. I tap the speaker button and put it to my ear, intent on finding out who's been tormenting me this entire time. "Hello?" I ask into the phone.

The clearing of a throat, a sigh, and some breathing is what greets me.

"Hello?" I ask again. "I know you're there because a) you picked up, and b) I can hear you breathing. So, who the fuck is this?"

My question is answered by the line clicking dead.

So, I decide to do what any rational person in my situation would do. I pull up my call log, jab the call button next to the number again and begin the game of patience all over again.

Eventually, they'll have to tell me who the fuck they are and I'm willing to sit on this bench for however long it takes.

EIGHTEEN

Vibrations Aren't Always Fun

THE AGITATOR

The phone won't stop buzzing, but I've got it shoved between my legs to keep the sound muffled. Eventually he'll have to give up, stop calling, and get back on the road.

What the fuck am I thinking?

Of course he won't give up. If he has even the slightest idea that it's irritating me, he'll keep doing it. He's Lakyn's spawn after all, and he has the same awe-inspiring and irritating self-confidence. I could see it in the smirk in his photo, and I've read it in every text... and now I've heard it in his voice.

He's a kid, but somehow his voice sent the same thrill down my back as Lakyn's. There's just something about that nonchalant, confident tone that makes me think twice about what I'm doing.

Hearing him was why I answered the call though. I

just wanted to know what he sounded like, to add it to the steadily building idea I have of him in my head. He's so much like his father, but more innocent in some ways. Still too naïve about the world, and about the monster that fathered him. Yet, there's no denying the paternity now.

Everything lines up, like little dominos in a row, and I've already knocked over the first one. Whether or not he'll ultimately be able to stand against Lakyn is still in question.

At least he's on his way here, not fast enough for my liking, because Ohio isn't close at all... but he's coming.

I hear movement in the other room and reach between my thighs to press the power button and decline the call.

The way my phone keeps vibrating from every call Aftyn makes is kind of entertaining, but I don't need anyone asking who the hell is calling me back to back. Everyone is allowed to have secrets, and this is one I plan on keeping until the grand reveal.

I'm not sure if my actions are some kind of vengeance, petty jealousy over his enigmatic nature, or just me seeking something fun in the never-ending void my life has become. Post-Lakyn Meyer no one is the same, and I'm definitely changed. For better or worse.

Well, let's be honest, it's definitely for the worse.

Barely a few seconds pass between calls, and this time I just let it vibrate. My voicemail is nothing but the automated repeat of my number, and eventually he'll get bored and move on. Just like Lakyn always does.

I do wish I'd been able to find out more about the mother though. Who was she? How the hell did she survive an evening with the man behind that heartbreaker grin and those perfectly blue eyes?

From what I understand, getting picked up by Lakyn Meyer is one of the last things a long list of women have done. Apart from the screaming and bleeding. So... why her? What was so special about this random bitch that she not only deserved to live, but was allowed to carry his seed to term?

Because now it's out there, walking around, driving ever closer to Arizona, and looking so much like its father that I found the resemblance eerie.

A noise in the next room makes me reach down and decline the call again, ending the vibration—but it almost instantly starts up again.

This little asshole is definitely Lakyn's kid, and while I appreciate his sudden urge to communicate, I don't feel like fucking up my life quite yet.

Sneaking the phone into my hands, I tap out a quick text: *We'll talk soon. Shouldn't you be on your way? Daddy's waiting.*

Locking the phone, I hold down the power button

to turn it off. I like the little back and forth we've had, but I'm going to draw lines with Aftyn that I was never able to with Lakyn. We'll communicate on my terms, on my timeline, and no childish behavior is going to make me change my mind.

NINETEEN

A Friend in Need

WILLA

I've been quietly watching Aftyn from the front seat of my vehicle. I had managed to get some sleep until he slammed the door when he got out. It jostled me awake but I had a feeling that pretending to still be lost in a slumber I knew he was longing for would be best.

I'm pretty sure that Daphne is still knocked out behind me because her breathing is heavy and even. *What I wouldn't give to not hear her breathing at all, ever again,* I think with an eye roll as I shift a little in the front seat.

Aftyn suddenly stands up from where he's been sitting at the bench. He looks wide awake now and completely pissed off so I decide to continue my façade of sleeping and close my eyes as much as I can to allow me just enough room to continue to watch him.

He slides his phone into his pocket, rubs his face irritably and looks up at the night sky. Something—or rather someone—seems to be bothering him, but he'll be good and goddamned if he lets that little secret out when I'm awake.

Aftyn likes to wear the mask of nonchalance. He likes to let me believe that nothing really bothers him after his mother was taken care of.

He said that everything that could ever hurt him had died with her and that he knew he'd be able to live a happy, productive life after that.

Apparently, he was wrong.

There are still buttons to press on Aftyn Meyer and someone knows exactly what pressure points to go after.

I watch him as he rubs the back of his neck with such force that I'm worried he'll either snap it or take the skin off. But he relents after a few seconds and begins to make his way back to the SUV.

I take a deep breath and do my best to mimic the sleeping bitch it the backseat's breathing pattern, but it sounds much too forced.

And I know that Aftyn will pick up on it right away.

'*What do I do?*' I wonder frantically as he opens the driver's side door then climbs in. At the angle I'm curled up in, I can't see his face anymore, but I can feel the frustration emanating from him.

It's almost like waves of white, hot anger are permeating from him and attempting to strangle everyone in the truck. Including him.

"God, I wish you were awake, Wills," he says softly

as the keys jingle. A few seconds later, the engine is brought back to life and the vehicle starts moving again.

———

I let out a low growl when the sun comes blaring through the windshield. I hadn't meant to fall asleep again because I could hear the hurt in Aftyn's tone when he got back in the truck, but I guess I was playing the sleeping beauty role much better than I thought I was.

"Finally awake?"

I sit up and untangle my legs from beneath myself, press my palms against the dashboard, and stretch as best as I can before I open my eyes and look at him.

He's giving me a friendly smile, which has been few and far between since this trip started, and I return the gesture.

If Aftyn needs anything in his life right now, it's kindness, and I'll do my best to give it to him until we see this to the end.

"Sorry," I reply in a tone still thick with sleep. Aftyn chuckles as he turns his eyes back toward the road. "I didn't mean to sleep for so long, Aftyn."

"It's okay. I plan on catching up on my sleep for the next thousand or so miles, so it's best that you're nice and rested up," he teases as he reaches up into the visor for his pack of cigarettes. "Fuck," he mumbles when he shakes it. It's empty and having seen Aftyn without nicotine before, I know that the best thing to do is find the nearest gas station.

"We're probably due for a fuel up," I say as I use my hands to brush back my hair.

"Yeah. Almost on E."

"Okay; hold on," I say as I reach down for my purse to retrieve my phone. Stifling a yawn, I tap on the screen then pull up the navigation application. I type in 'gas stations near me' and settle on the very first one that pops up. "Take the next exit," I instruct him as I sit back in my chair and recline it a little. I don't plan on falling asleep again, but my body is so goddamn cramped right now that I know I need to allow some kind of room to stretch my limbs in.

"Lead the way, Magellan," Aftyn jokes, and I turn my face toward him and smile. He seems to be trying for a good day today and I'll do my best to make sure that he has one—regardless of the mood he puts me in sometimes.

After we exit the highway, it takes ten minutes until we reach the gas station with me giving him direction ahead of the navigation. Once I see the sign, I point it out and he nods as he pulls in.

"Here," I begin as I reach down for my purse again, "you fill the tank and I'll go get you a couple of cartons." Aftyn nods as he takes my debit card. "And don't leave me here, Meyer," I tell him before I hop out of the truck and head into the small food mart attached to the gas station.

"Leave you behind? What the fuck would I do without you, Wills?" he shouts after me. I glance at him over my shoulder and stick my tongue out to which he laughs and shakes his head.

A bell dings somewhere inside of the mart when I pull the door open. I walk toward the back of the place and grab numerous bags of chips of different varieties. I grab some candy bars and head to the register to dump them on the counter before I go back to the snacks and grab a hand full of *Slim Jims*, which just so happen to be Aftyn's favorite thing to munch on. One more trip to grab a few bottles of water and I think I'm done with the bare necessities.

The guy behind the counter chuckles as he begins to ring everything up. "Anything else?" he asks me kindly as he begins to put my items into a plastic bag.

"Um, yeah," I say as I get to my tiptoes and crane my neck. "I need a couple of cartons of those."

I reach into my wallet and toss my ID on the counter because I just know he's going to ask for it. Once he's satisfied that I'm of age to buy the cigarettes, we complete the transaction and I head back out into the morning sun.

I wonder where we are, I think as I reach into the bag and pull out a candy bar. I pull the wrapper back and begin to nibble on it when I suddenly realize that I don't see Aftyn anymore.

"Great," I mumble to myself as I walk a little faster toward the truck.

When I get close enough, I see that he has the hatch open in the back so I walk around and nudge him to scoot over.

"Here," I say as I hand him the cartons.

"Thanks, Wills," he replies quietly.

"Look in the bag," I tell him with a nod as I place it between us. "I got you something."

Aftyn raises an eyebrow curiously as he peeks into the bag then looks at me with a grin. "See? You're not so bad when you wanna be nice."

"Thanks, Meyer," I reply with an eye roll. Backhanded compliments are something I'm used to when it comes to Aftyn, but since starting this trip, he's been a little down, so instead of sniping back at him, I let him win this round.

"What's got you down?" I ask him, deciding that beating around the bush isn't going to make him feel any better.

Aftyn shrugs as he opens one of the *Slim Jims* and begins to chew on it.

"Is it because we're getting closer?" I press gently.

He shrugs again and I decide that maybe it's best to let this conversation go for now. He'll tell me what he wants me to know when he's ready and I'll be the friend to him I was the same day we took care of his mother.

"We should probably keep going," I say as I get to my feet. "Give me the keys, I'll drive from here."

Aftyn doesn't look up to meet my eyes, instead he just hands over the keys without so much as a word and stands up, closes the hatch behind him, and walks over to the passenger side of the truck.

Once he's safely tucked inside, I begin to make my way toward the driver's side door, stopping long enough to peer in at Daphne who's now wide awake, eyes forward, and in a world of her fucking own again.

Soon.

TWENTY

Pushing Buttons

DAPHNE

I never sleep very deeply. Probably a consequence of my fantastic childhood and all the wonderful things that have happened since I left that shithole, but it has a few benefits. One of them is that I'm pretty damn hard to sneak up on, and the second is that I'm a solid fake sleeper when I need to be.

Of course, I get a lot of practice hitchhiking around.

Decent guys will let you sleep if they think you've passed out in their car, the bad ones will almost always try something. It's a quick and efficient way of figuring out whose car I'm in... usually.

With Aftyn and Willa things are more difficult. These two just don't talk about things with each other. They dance around topics, trying not to step on each other's toes while simultaneously launching snarky comments at random. When he pulled into that rest stop along the highway to lay on a picnic table for a while, Willa pretended to be asleep while she watched him, and continued faking it when he climbed back in and basically called her out by saying he wished she was awake. I was sure she'd sit up, happy to feel needed, but the bitch had just laid there against the window. It's an odd dichotomy, but I think I've figured out what's going on with them. Just friends, nothing more, even if one or both of them are physically attracted enough to fuck around occasionally.

And that's good news for me, because I haven't had a decent fuck in too long, and Aftyn looks like he would be a lot of fun. It will just depend on if he makes a move or not, although he already made the first move by approaching me in the parking lot and defending me against the bitch currently driving the car.

Sitting up straight, I hear the crack of a water bottle from the front seat and realize how dry my mouth feels. "Um, any chance I could have some water?"

"Sure." Aftyn tosses me an unopened bottle and I catch it just as Willa huffs.

"I bought those for us," she grumbles, and I take great joy in twisting off the top to drink.

Half the bottle is gone before I feel like my thirst is slaked enough to poke the bear. "I would have bought some stuff if I'd known we were stopping, but I didn't realize you'd gone inside already when I woke up."

A lie since I'd woken up as soon as the car started slowing down, but it'll just make my next sleeping attempt more convincing.

"You have money?" Willa asks, glancing at me in the mirror for a second, the doubt in her tone more than clear.

"Yeah. Why? Do you want me to pay you back for the water?" I hold it up, but she just rolls her eyes, not engaging in an argument, and Aftyn doesn't seem up for conversation either. "Okaaaaay. Well, thanks for the water. Why are you guys heading to Arizona?"

"It's personal," Willa answers at the same time Aftyn says, "Going to see someone."

Neither of them are going to budge on that topic, yet, but I have a feeling they'll react to my next conversation change.

"Did you know you've got blood back here?" I ask, and the car jerks slightly as Willa tries to turn and look. Aftyn actually sits up in the front seat, twisting to scan the space, and I point toward the opposite window. When his blue eyes land on the dull red smear, a wicked smirk slides over his lips.

"Look at that. Maybe I do owe you a car detail, Wills," he says, facing her again.

"Where is there blood?"

"On the panel by the window. Seems like Dexter left behind more than just fond memories with us for our road trip." Aftyn sounds like he's almost laughing, and it feels contagious because I'm smiling before I even realize it.

"We should have taken him to one of those ER places." Willa shakes her head, her thumb tapping an impatient rhythm on the steering wheel. "Can you call him on my phone? I just want to check on him. If he has a concussion, he really shouldn't go to sleep."

"Stop trying to be his mother."

"I'm not!" Willa snaps, holding out her hand. "Just give me my phone if you don't want to talk to him."

"No, you're driving. Be a responsible adult and drive so I can get some fucking sleep."

"The responsible thing to do would have been stopping to get him checked out, Aftyn, but you didn't want to delay the trip because you're so fucking selfish!" Willa tries to grab for her purse, but Aftyn must have moved it out of reach because she suddenly smacks the steering wheel and lets out a little frustrated screech. "This is your fault, you know? We could have just got Dexter some help, but you wanted him to suffer. You've never liked him and I don't get it. He's practically in love with you."

"Yawn, Willa. You're not telling me anything you haven't already told me in another one of your hormonal bitchfits." The sound of something clunking into the floorboard against a plastic bag is clear over the low music. "I'm not letting you call him while you're driving, and you should just enjoy the break. Your precious charity case will be waiting for you to save the day again and again when you get back."

"You call him then!" Willa shouts, and Aftyn scoffs.

"No way, it'll just encourage the little asshole."

"I'll do it." For a second I thought I was too quiet,

but they both go silent and Willa's eyes meet mine in the rearview.

"Give her the phone, Aftyn."

"Oh, so you don't trust her enough to sit quietly in the backseat, but now it's okay to give her access to all your nudes? Your Facebook account? Your filthy text messages between you and whatever boy toys you're stringing along around New York?" Aftyn laughs. "You're a fucking case, Wills."

"Either you give her the phone or I'm taking the next exit and turning us around to head home so I can *personally* check on Dexter."

"You won't do that," Aftyn says, and this time it's Willa's turn to laugh.

"Oh really? Try me."

"You don't understand," Aftyn continues, leaning across the center console to plant a hand on Willa's knee. "You won't turn us around because if you think I'm going to *let* you turn us around, you need to take a minute and remember who the fuck is sitting next to you."

"Aftyn, stop." Willa's tone has an edge of panic, and I can feel the SUV accelerating. Leaning forward, I realize Aftyn is pushing her leg down, forcing her foot to the floor with an iron grip just above her knee. She swerves around a car, and then another before we have a bit of empty space ahead of us again. "AFTYN!"

"Don't threaten me, Willa. We both know it's hollow, and I really don't like it when you push my buttons." He sounds completely calm, and I know I should probably be terrified as we get closer and closer to the next car ahead... but I'm not scared. My heart is racing, and my skin feels like it's humming, but this is excitement not fear. Everything feels more real, like someone reached into my brain and turned up the color, the sound, the entire texture of the world.

"You're right, okay? I wasn't serious, just let go of my fucking leg! You're going to kill us!" Willa says, her voice sped up with panic, and I can see the pulse thumping just below her jaw, making her skin bounce.

"Say you're sorry," Aftyn whispers, leaning closer to her, his lips almost brushing that spot on her neck I can't look away from.

"I'm sorry!" she shouts, and he drags his tongue over her skin, flicking her earring with the tip of his tongue before he finally releases her. Willa lets go of the gas, and the car begins to slow down as Aftyn drops back into his seat.

"That's why you'll always lose, Wills."

"What are you talking about?" she asks, bringing the car back into normal speed range.

He turns his head to look at her, and I shift in my seat just so I can see his eyes. They're almost sleepy, still so relaxed as he says, "When it comes to the two of us, I'll always win because you're afraid to die... and I'm not."

Willa doesn't say anything in response and, judging by the white-knuckle grip she has on the steering wheel, I'm pretty sure she's still trying to come down from the panic. Personally, I'm disappointed that the show is over so quickly. but it's Aftyn's last comment that has me biting down on my lip to hide the smile the words summon.

"Here you go, Daphne," Aftyn says, holding the designer purse over his shoulder, and I take it from him. "Her phone is in there somewhere, but feel free to dig around for anything you might want. I'm sure she's got some cash in her wallet, a spare credit card or two."

I can tell by just how tense Willa's shoulders are that she hates me holding her purse, but she doesn't have the balls to speak up against Aftyn right now. It only takes a second to locate her phone, a brand-new iPhone with a shimmery blue case. When I tap the screen, it tries to read my face but obviously doesn't unlock. "I need your code."

"Hand it to me," Willa grits out between clenched teeth, reaching back over her shoulder, but Aftyn snags her wrist and shoves her hand back into her lap.

"No phones while driving, Wills."

Taking a deep breath, Willa rolls her neck from side to side before she finally answers quietly. "Eight, zero, four, one."

"Thanks," I tell her, unlocking the phone with the code before I scroll to her contacts and find 'Dexter' with a little heart emoji next to his name in her favorites. Tapping it, the phone starts ringing, but it barely gets through a full ring before the voicemail picks up. The kid sounds young, awkward, and I listen to the end of his pathetic message before I end the call. "It went straight to voicemail. Do you want me to... leave him a message?"

"No," Willa snaps, and I flip to the photos out of curiosity while she glares out the front windshield. There are a handful of risqué photos, but I'm more curious about the ones she's taken of Aftyn. I click on them at random, moving quickly, but eventually I find one where he's not looking at her. He's sitting at a table, looking to the side, and he's got that smirk on his face that makes me want to know more about him.

Willa is annoyingly two-dimensional, but Aftyn isn't. He's got layers. Complexity.

And I want to see more of it.

I just have to figure out what buttons to push with them next.

TWENTY-ONE

Perchance to Dream

AFTYN

I reach into the backseat and snatch Willa's phone out of Daphne's hand. She's had enough time to snoop around, and in all honesty, I just wanted to piss of my best friend which is completely different than invading her privacy.

After I push the button to lock Wills' phone again, I lean into the back and smack Daphne's hand when I find her rifling through her purse. She looks up at me with an arched eyebrow, amusement on her face, and I ignore it all as I retrieve the bag and toss it on the floor between my feet.

I run a hand back through my hair, the taste of Willa's salty skin still on my tongue as I close my eyes and fold an arm behind my head.

The bitchfest can continue after I've gotten some sleep.

I'll be well rested and better prepared to fight her then.

"Where did you go after school you little shit?"

I take a step back against the door as Mom storms into the living room to screech at me. I'm not allowed to do anything in this house that she doesn't approve of, and she's never wanted me to have friends. She hates me, hates Willa, and constantly compares me to my "son-of-a-bitch" father. A man I don't even know who holds some kind of sway over the both of us.

Her because she can't seem to let him go and me because I apparently look so much like him.

"I walked Willa home," I tell her defensively. I never lied to my mother before and her being this angry won't change that. I'm not a liar; I hate liars and when the truth is readily available, there's no reason for a fallacy to pass through my lips.

"You just think you're hot shit because your balls finally dropped, don't you?" she barks at me, raising a finger and pointing it in my face. "You're going to be like that no-good father of yours—I can see it now."

I clear my throat and try to stay calm. I'm sick and tired of constantly bearing the brunt of misdeeds done to her by someone I don't even know.

"Sorry," I mumble, my eyes lowering to the floor. "I

should have called to tell you that I wouldn't be home right away."

It's not fair.

Everyone else gets to have friends except for me. Willa is a nice girl; she's got lots of money too and sometimes, we skip the cafeteria swill for a really good lunch a few blocks away from the high school.

"Keep your dick in your pants, Aftyn. Don't make me cut it off," Mom warns me in a low, serious tone.

My lower lip trembles as I quickly wipe away a tear. I'm not afraid of anyone, not even Mom, but I know she's serious because she hates me so goddamn much.

And even though I know this will cost me later, I do the only thing that I know will make me feel safe for a little while.

I mumble another apology as I walk by her and head for my room. I close the door gently behind me, but make sure that the lock is in place before I reach under my bed and grab an empty backpack. I immediately begin stuffing a few days worth of clothes and underwear in it, grab a stick of deodorant off my old, broken down dresser, and a brush. Once I'm as packed as I can be, I head over to the window of my bedroom and climb out.

I know Willa will spot me a toothbrush and if she doesn't have an extra, she'll buy me one and I'll pay her back for it somehow.

I just need to get as far away from being this hated as I can.

"Fuck!"

I sit up with a start and a shout, causing Willa to swerve the truck.

"Jesus Christ, Aftyn! A little warning before you start yelling, huh?" she says in a trembling voice.

I blow out my breath and wipe the sweat from my palms on the legs of my jeans. Rubbing the side of my neck, I glare at her.

"Sorry; the next time I have a nightmare, I'll be sure to be more concerned about your reaction to it than my own," I snipe at her.

Willa shakes her head, eyes still on the road, as she reaches a hand over and rests it on my leg.

"I'm sorry about that, honey," she says quietly. "I didn't know you were having nightmares again."

"Neither did I," I reply heavily as I reach down for her hand. Our fingers interlace as my leg begins to jump rapidly in place. The only thing that can usually calm me down after a nightmare is Wills. Be it sitting around silently in the same room, holding her hand, or just calling her and listening to her breathing.

"Are you two fucking?" Daphne suddenly asks from the back seat.

"Mind your goddamn business," Wills snaps back, with a narrow-eyed glare in the rearview mirror.

I grit my teeth.

Maybe I should have left this roadkill at the

fucking rest area where she belonged because the bickering between the two of them is starting to grate on my nerves.

"Ignore her," I say to Wills, quietly. "I plan to."

Willa steals a glance in my direction, a smirk on her lips as she squeezes my hand. It's not that I plan on letting Daphne off on the next stop—I haven't fucked or fooled around with her yet, so the thought alone would be preposterous—I just want her to shut the fuck up for now so I can get my head back on straight.

After that, the two of them can go back to verbally assailing each other. Maybe even physically. *I wonder what Wills would look like oiled up and slapping the shit out of Daphne?*

I shift slightly in my seat and move Willa's hand closer to my inner thigh. The thought that crept into my mind caused the blood flow to head South and maybe she'd be willing to—

"Really, Aftyn?" she asks with a shake of her head. She immediately pulls her hand out of my mine as she leans her elbow against the window and rests the side of her face in the palm of her hand. "Seems like your fine now."

I chuckle as I glance out the window, resting my head against the cool pane. The trees go by rapidly and I even see a small doe walking along the side of the highway as it grazes.

I can't help that I happen to be the way that I am, and I know that if we didn't have someone else in the backseat, she would have at the very least jerked me off.

Willa reaches over and taps my thigh. When I look at her, she nods toward the windshield and I follow her eyes.

Welcome to Indiana. Crossroads of America.

I close my eyes as I nestle back in the seat and hope that the closer we get, the less I'll have the same fucking nightmares every time I try to go to sleep.

Because even though Mom hated Lakyn, she seemed afraid of him finding us all the same.

TWENTY-TWO

Nightmares and Watersports

WILLA

I keep looking over at Aftyn while he dozes, waiting for another nightmare to wake him. It's been a long time since he had nightmares about his whore of a mother, but whenever they start up... they always keep coming.

He's already had two today, and I'm sure more are on the way. The nightmares are relentless, just like she was.

But it's probably his own damn fault he's having them again. We're on this insane road trip to meet his dad, who was the only one person Aftyn's mom hated more than him.

Lakyn.

She used to compare Aftyn to him all the time, scream terrible things, even though Aftyn had no control over who knocked her up. It wasn't his fault she's always been a whore, and that whichever john managed to get her pregnant didn't hang around long enough for her to even pee on a stick.

I never put much stock in the shit his mom said about Aftyn reminding her of the man, but now that I've seen his photo... I can't deny the resemblance. It's almost creepy. And I'm sure the only reason she even knew which dick Aftyn belonged to was because of just how similar he looks to his dad.

"Where are we?" Aftyn grumbles, waking up and stretching. Sometimes I swear he can read my mind, like he knows when I'm thinking about him, but I'd never admit that to him.

"Just hit Missouri." I only glance over for a second before I look back at the highway, but I saw enough. His shirt is halfway up his abs from the contorted stretch he's pulling off in the passenger seat, and I know if he sees me looking, he'll make a thing of it, so I do my best to distract him. "I'm surprised you didn't wake up when we were going through St. Louis."

"We're already through Indiana?" he asks, sitting up straight and staring out the windshield like he's not sure he believes me.

"And the bottom part of Illinois," I add, and he scrubs at his face.

"Damn, Wills. You're making good time." Grinning, he tilts his head to the side to look at me. "Have my driving skills finally rubbed off on you?"

"Not at all." Laughing, I shove his fingers off my knee so I can focus on the road, and he sighs like me rebuffing him is something new. It's practically a running gag with us now, especially on this road trip when he hasn't been able to keep his hands to himself whenever he isn't in the driver's seat.

He's too easily bored.

I've always thought that about him. If the topic isn't him, or if it doesn't directly involve him, then Aftyn is most likely not paying attention. After another stretch, he settles against the window for a minute or two, but I jump when he suddenly jolts forward in his seat and shouts, "Exit here!"

"Where?" I ask, slapping his hand away when he grabs for the steering wheel, making us swerve for a second. "Are you fucking crazy?"

"There! Hurry up and exit!" He's pointing at a big sign that says 'Mark Twain National Forest,' and I merge over.

"I'm going!" I snap, but I'm apparently not moving fast enough for him, because he goes for the wheel again. I manage to block his arm as I get in the lane for the exit, gritting my teeth against a scream of frustration. "Chill the fuck out, Aftyn! Do you want us to crash?"

"You almost missed it, Wills. Come on. I just want to be able to stretch my legs... and maybe some other things." Aftyn grins at me again, but I just roll my eyes as I take the ramp off the highway, following the signs to the entrance of the National Forest.

The bitch in the backseat is awake now, sitting up

and looking around like the idiot she is, and I start to think that this forest might not be a bad idea. It would be so easy to 'forget' her—or knock her unconscious and leave her in the woods. I'd just have to get Aftyn distracted. Make him forget about her long enough for us to be back on the highway, too far down the road to turn back for the roadside tramp.

"Hell yes, this is exactly what we need." Aftyn rolls the window down, sticking his head out as we turn onto a central road into the forest.

"Where do you want to stop?" I ask, smiling at him as he hangs out the side of my car like there's nothing else on his mind. So much better than his post-nightmare panic.

"Keep going. I don't want to be able to hear the highway." Pointing to the right at a fork in the road, he says, "Go that way."

"Okay." Shrugging, I follow his directions a few more times until the road gets a little rougher. It's still paved, but much narrower and definitely not as smooth as the main one. The trees are closer too, and I'm not sure if we meet a car going the other way if I can pull off enough to let them pass. "See the right spot to stretch your legs yet?"

He's silent for another minute or so, leaned forward on the dash, until I finally see a smile spread across his face.

"There. Park up there." Aftyn points ahead of us,

and I know exactly why he's chosen it. There's a little wooden sign that says 'LAKE' with an arrow pointing to the left. Parking the car in a flat area to the side of the narrow road, I turn it off and Aftyn jumps out immediately.

"You happy?" I ask through his open window and Aftyn's bright blue eyes focus on me.

"How about you and I have some solo time, Wills? That's what this road trip was supposed to be, right?"

Glancing at the bitch in the backseat, I grin and nod at him. "Yeah. Just us."

"Come on then!" he shouts at me before leaning into his window to look at Daphne. "You stay here. Watch the car or whatever."

"Okay," she answers, pulling her sweet idiot act again. I don't trust her at all though, and I'm hoping she wanders off somewhere while we're walking around.

If she wanders straight into traffic? Even better.

Reaching down into the passenger footwell, I grab my purse, the snacks, and the last bottle of water. She can fucking fend for herself if she wants something.

"Feel free to leave," I tell her, climbing out of the car before she has the chance to respond as I shove the water and my keys into my purse.

When I turn around, Aftyn is spinning in circles, his face turned up to the pale gray sky. It doesn't look like it will rain, but the sun definitely isn't showing its face today. Still, he hasn't looked this happy in a long time, and it makes me smile.

"You ready, Wills?" he asks, turning toward the path that leads to the lake, and I'm so relieved to be away from Daphne that I shove the snacks into his hands and run right past him.

"Race you!"

"You bitch!" he shouts, but he's laughing as I sprint toward the lake. The path takes longer than I expected though, and eventually I start to run out of steam, slowing down enough for him to grab me around the waist as he slams into my back. "GOT YOU!"

Shoving him off, I laugh as he throws an arm around my shoulder, pulling me right back against his side.

"Okay, Aftyn, you got me. You win. Now, where the hell is this lake supposed to be?" I ask, untangling myself from him again as we both breathe hard, scanning the trees.

"Path leads that way, so..." Aftyn shrugs, still grinning as he walks backward for a few steps. "Come on, Wills. Where's your sense of adventure?"

He lets out a war cry as he turns around, heading toward the lake at a much faster pace than I'm in the mood for. I already ran this far, and who the fuck knows how far this stupid lake is? Even if we don't find it, the trees are dense enough to give me that feeling of being secluded, and I like it.

Not that I'd enjoy actually camping out here all

night… but the occasional pass through nature is nice. Refueling. Something we both need on this ridiculous road trip.

"Found it!" Aftyn shouts, and I walk a little faster until I finally catch sight of the lake over the edge of a hill. The water isn't all I see though. Aftyn already has his shirt off and he's working at his pants as he spots me on the path. "Get your clothes off, Wills. Let's take a dip."

"I am *not* skinny dipping with you. You can't keep your hands to yourself when I'm dressed." Crossing my arms, I watch him as he kicks his shoes to the side, dropping his pants before removing his socks too. Standing in just his boxers, I can't deny just how good Aftyn looks… but I'm still not fucking him.

If I ever actually gave in, I'm pretty confident that would be the end of our friendship. And, even though he's an asshole most of the time, I actually value the connection we have.

"Keep your underwear on then, just get in the damn water with me." Stepping closer, Aftyn cranks up the charm, giving me wicked puppy dog eyes as he holds out a hand for me. "Come on. It's just us."

That is what does me in. The fact that he made that bitch Daphne stay behind so we could spend some time together. Alone. Without her irritating commentary.

"Fine, but I'm keeping my underwear and my bra on," I say, tugging my shirt over my head.

"Your choice to sit in the car in wet clothes!" Aftyn laughs, running for the edge of the lake, sending up huge splashes when he collides with the water. Before I even have my jeans unbuttoned, Aftyn's gone. Diving under the water with more grace than he deserves to have. A second later he pops up, sending water flying again as he laughs. "This feels amazing, Wills. Get your ass in here!"

I ignore his taunts as I strip down to my bra and underwear, folding everything on top of my shoes to try and keep bugs out of my clothes. I've got dry underwear and another bra in my bag, but I'll have to completely strip to change. Wavering over keeping them on or not, I groan when Aftyn whistles at me.

"Hurry up! You are so fucking slow," he calls out.

"You're too fucking impatient!" Turning around, I decide to keep them on as I move to the edge of the lake. It's bigger than I thought it would be, and there's no way I'm just charging into the water like him. It still has a chill to it, and as the water gets above my knees, I know it's going to take my breath away.

"Just dive in, Wills. It'll be way easier to adjust."

"Not all of us jump headfirst into absolutely everything," I snark, taking my time as the water reaches my hips. My plan is to wait here so I can adjust to it, but Aftyn suddenly bursts out of the water next to me. Before I can stop him, he scoops me up and tosses me farther out into the lake. I scream something at him just before I go under, the chill pushing the rest of my air out as I bounce back up from the bottom.

"Dammit, Aftyn!" I shout as soon as I get my head above water again, but he's just laughing, floating on his back a few yards away. "God, you're such an asshole."

"We don't have all day for you to be a princess about the water, Willa."

Splashing him, I roll my eyes, but I know it's a mistake the second he looks at me. Aftyn is upright in a flash, that sly grin tilting his lips just before he swings his arm across the top of the water to send a wall of water at my face.

"You ass!" Wiping my face, I lean back and float so I can kick water right back at him. Soon enough we're in a full-on water war, but Aftyn is definitely winning. He keeps going under just so he can pick me up and throw me.

If I had any make-up left before this, it's definitely gone now... but as our laughter winds down, I don't even care. It's been way too long since Aftyn and I just hung out together without some alternate agenda for one or both of us.

Of course, I'm already driving him to Arizona in my car... but it's still nice.

Both of us just floating, his hand reaching out to find mine so that we can link our fingers and stay together while the clouds roll by in a never-ending heather gray blanket.

This moment—this moment right now—makes the entire shitshow of a trip worth it, because for once Aftyn isn't putting on a show or trying to be the biggest asshole in the room. It's just us.

Like it was always supposed to be.

TWENTY-THREE

Battleaxe pt. 2

AFTYN

Being in the lake alone with Wills, away from the absolute mess that is Daphne, feels a lot better than it should.

I know that eventually we'll be able to ditch her and I'm hoping that it's before we get to Lakyn's.

I'm still not entirely sure how I'll react to seeing him in person, but I'm sure it will be better than how I would react to seeing Mom every day.

"What's wrong, Aftyn?" Wills asks, pushing my damp hair away from my forehead.

"Huh?" I ask distractedly.

"You've got that Meyer scowl happening so..."

I chuckle as I do my best to force a smile onto my face, though from the way she squeezes my hand, I know that I've only deepened the scowl.

"Thinking about Mom," I tell her as I look back up

at the sky. *God, I wish it would rain. Drowning in the lake right now with my best friend would put Romeo and Juliet to shame.*

"Well don't," she says as she moves closer to me and wraps an arm around my waist. Wills places her head against my chest, and I breathe her in, completely intoxicated by her scent and the freshwater all around us. "She always puts you in a bad mood, and I think we've both had enough attitudes on this trip to last the rest of the way."

Normally, when I make a move on Willa, it's calculated and there's been plenty of thought put behind it. The bitch packs a mean swing and I know that I always have to be in a position to dodge it, but...

"Hey," I say softly.

Willa looks up at me with a curious look in her eyes, and a smile on her lips. I get it; she thinks that she's already calmed me down, but just once I'd like to know what she tastes like without having to fight for it.

Taking a deep breath, I lower my lips against hers and hold her against me.

The sliver of time between us brings forth a maelstrom of emotions in me that I didn't even know I had for her.

"Fuck off, Aftyn!" she barks, shoving me away roughly and destroying the moment before I've even had a chance to fully embrace it—and her.

I throw my hands up in the air before I turn away

from her and swim a few yards away. Turning on my back, I decide to float for a little bit, glancing up at the sky when I know that the only way to get Willa to understand that it's always ever been us—and should be—is to tell her a story.

A smirk creases my lips as I begin.

"You know, sometimes I wonder why you're such a bitch but then I remember that precious princesses that have had life handed to them on silver platters, with those silver spoons crammed down their throats like an old rich man's cock, is usually what does it."

"I'm not going to argue with you," she snaps, cutting me off, but I laugh and continue.

"I know you like to think that you know everything, Wills, but there's something you *don't* know. Curious? Or are you going to bitchfloat back to shore and wonder what I could have possibly told you right now?"

I lower my legs beneath the surface and run my hands back through my hair. I want to look her in the fucking eye when I tell her what really happened to her charity case, because she needs to remember who the fuck is in charge here, and it's definitely not her.

"I'm already bored," she remarks, rolling her eyes and turning her face away.

Not for long.

"Dexter didn't really catch a ride home," I begin conversationally. When Willa slowly starts to turn her eyes toward me again, it's my turn to look away and relish in knowing that I have her undivided fucking attention.

"What are you talking about?" she asks, a tremor of uncertainty to her tone.

"It's your fault, really," I continue as I wade a little further away from her. When I confess my sin to her, she's going to fucking explode. And while I don't mind having a go with her, I think it's a little more fun to have her chase me for it.

"What did you do, Aftyn?" she presses, her eyes starting to water.

"So, you'll cry for him but not for me? When was the last time you shed a tear for me, Wills? Was it when I would come over after school because Mom had taken a belt to me just for walking in five minutes late? Was it when she would ruin each and every birthday by telling me that she should have gotten rid of me when she had the chance? No; you always just told me that it would be okay and then we'd sit around and talk. Not *once* have you shed a fucking tear for me. I thought we were supposed to be besties. What's up with that?"

I know that I'm rambling now, but I'm so fucking fed up with always being someone's second thought and never their first, that if Willa does try to come after me right now, then we're going to have one hell of tango.

"Every fucking night when you would have to go

back to that hellhole!" she screams at me. "I never let you see me cry for you because I was supposed to be your fucking rock. I've cried for you more than I've cried for anyone else in my fucking life!"

"You can save those tears from now on, babe," I tell her with a bitter laugh. "Actually, no. Spill them all right now, I want to see you fucking cry. Isn't that how you're supposed to mourn, anyway? When someone dies, don't people show up at funerals crying like they actually gave a fuck in the first place? Sorry you couldn't attend Dexter's, but I didn't think that taking you into the bathroom after I left him in the fucking stall would have been so smart considering we were still close to New York. Gotta see my old man, ya know?"

Willa's lower lip begins to tremble instantly. I can see the disbelief in her eyes as the tears spill down her cheeks before she takes a deep breath and wades a little closer to me.

"You... you killed Dex?"

"Duh," I reply with a smirk.

Willa's face turns red with anger before she immediately turns away from me and starts swimming toward the shoreline. Probably with every intent on leaving me here, but I've always been bigger and faster than her, so I take a deep breath and put some strength into my strokes to follow her.

But as soon as she feels me catching up to her, she dives under the water, disappearing from the surface.

I stop moving and glance around. I have no idea where she's gone but if she thinks I'm just going to wait it out and hope for the best, she's out of her goddamn mind.

I begin moving toward shore again as quickly as I can, knowing that I have to reserve some energy for when I get there. Willa is pissed off and there's nothing that's going to keep her from trying to do me harm right now.

Which is fine by me.

It keeps the excitement in our friendship alive to have a little scuffle every now and then.

A few moments later, I see her pulling herself up on the shoreline. Nowhere near where we first walked into the lake, which means that I have to change—

Oh, they showed up at a really bad time, I think to myself as I watch a young couple wander toward the lake. The guy is carrying a white bucket in one hand and the chick is carrying a couple of fishing poles. But the one thing I notice the most is how they're holding hands like Wills and I tend to do sometimes before she remembers it's me then has a bitch fit about it.

I bob where I am for a little bit.

I want to watch the scene unfold because something tells me that it's going to be glorious.

The chick drops the fishing poles when she notices Wills and rushes over to probably ask if she's okay. Willa's shoulders are hunched, her face is in her hands, and she's sobbing.

Not for me, though.

Never for me.

The guy walks over to where his gal is standing, her hands on Willa's arms, trying her best to console her, not realizing that the little shit that's in front of her is probably deadlier than any wildlife that may be roaming the National Park.

Except for me.

That's why I know that I can't watch any longer and I have to get to Willa quickly. Even though she's out for my blood right now, I can't let anything happen to her —and I sure as fuck can't afford her babbling what I did to Dexter to these jamokes.

I crack my neck when I reach the shore. My feet become caked by the dirt as I start to make my way toward them, completely unforgiving in what I've done to Willa.

I've learned through trial and error, that sometimes, an emotional assault can do much more damage than a physical one.

"Wills," I call out when I'm close enough for her to hear me.

She pulls her arms out of the chick's grip and snaps her head up to glare at me with a hatred that I had only ever seen from Mom before.

And it makes me smile.

Because even though Willa loves me in her own, fucked up way, she can still hate me just as much, if not even more.

"We should probably head back up to the—"

"Who are you?" the guy asks, taking a menacing step toward me. Seems he wants to be the knight in shining armor right now. Protect two pussies for the price of one, but he's never met a dragon quite like me before.

"I hate you!" Willa suddenly screeches in a tone I've never heard from her. It's wrought with despair, heartbreak, and ire. Even in the state that she's in, it kinda warms my heart that she doesn't take it out on me.

She knocks the chick over with as much force as she can muster. The chick lets out a scream as Wills puts her hands around her throat and starts to slam her head into the ground. Her guy turns around instantly to try and save his pussy, but that's the only thing I needed.

A moment of distraction that causes him to forget that the dragon was still nearby.

I give him a kidney shot and when he hunches over in pain, I immediately loop an arm around his neck and pull him back against me. He's too busy trying to breathe to struggle too much, and that's just fine by me.

"I hate you! I hate you!" Willa keeps screaming as she continues to bash the chick's head into the dirt and pebbles.

I shift slightly behind Mr. Bad Ass because

watching Willa basically turn this bitch's head to mush is getting me hard.

When Willa finally lets go of the dead girl's throat, she gets to her feet shakily, and I tilt my head to admire her handywork.

"I think you missed a spot," I tell her dryly.

She snaps her eyes at me, her lip trembling even harder than before, then she walks over to the bucket a few inches away from us. Reaching inside, she retrieves a folding bowie knife.

I take a step back and bring my human shield with me.

Nothing about the look in her eyes right now gives me confidence about what she's thinking.

Maybe if I dribble a little white lie to let her know that he died happy, then—

A loud gurgle suddenly escapes from the guy that I've been using to protect myself from her.

A warm rush of something pooling at my feet and I know that Willa is nowhere near satisfied with the blood she's spilled.

"I'm going to fucking kill you," she seethes at me as she places a hand on the guy's shoulder, right next to my forearm.

I take a deep breath and wait for the moment to present itself. And when it does, I push him toward Willa and take a few steps back.

I quickly scoop up one of the fishing poles and use my teeth to snap the wire so that I can roll it around my fist, making sure that the hook is at the top and wait.

I'm faster than Willa, but she's more cunning, which means this may potentially suck more than it should.

Suddenly, her face crumples as she lets out another wail.

I tense my body and wait.

Trusting her right now is not a fucking option and I still need to get to Arizona.

With or without Willa.

She drops to her knees, looks at the dying man next to her, then sets her rage on him. She raises the knife and plunges it into him, over and over, the sound is wet, sick, and fucking all-consuming.

It's making me hard again.

I lower my guard when she's finally done. She drops the knife to the side, her hands completely soaked in blood as it continues to slowly ooze out of the gaping wounds she's made in his torso. I crane my neck to take a better look and shake my head in appreciation.

She's stabbed him so many fucking times that if she had any more strength left in her, she would have easily reached his spine. I can see his insides, or what's left of them, and I can see what pure anguish can do to someone who thinks their invincible.

And maybe now, I'll have her on my side once and for all.

"Come on," I tell her quietly as I reach down and extend a hand toward her. She lets me pull her to her feet and I push her hair behind her ear, using a thumb to wipe away a blood-soaked tear. "We need to get cleaned up before we head out again."

TWENTY-FOUR

Collecting Knives and Memories

DAPHNE

I wait in the car until I see Aftyn and Willa disappear into the trees, running with each other like a couple of pre-teen best friends. Straight out of some awkward 1950s idealized version of Americana—*obnoxious.*

Rolling my eyes, I grab my backpack, make sure it's all zipped up, and then I get out of the car and slam the door. The boom of the door closing seems louder in the silence of the woods, and I take a deep breath and lean back to look up at the sky. It's overcast, dismal, which means if I don't find another ride, I'm gonna get soaked.

One problem at a time.

Wandering into the woods on the opposite side of the road from where the two loveless not-lovers went, I go deep enough into the trees that if another car goes by they won't see me peeing behind a tree. Not that it *really* matters. If I'm lucky, some idiot will drive by and

I can make up a story about getting left behind by my friends.

Not that I've ever actually made any friends.

As soon as I'm done, I stand back up and button my jeans, tugging on the backpack straps as I get it adjusted on my shoulders before I start walking. I'm not heading back to the highway yet. As strange as the pair of them are, I agree with Aftyn that being out here feels good. Being cramped in their damn car for a day has been pretty shitty, and even though I tried to have some fun with them... they clearly don't want to play.

Too busy baiting each other into sexually charged arguments to give two shits about the girl they *chose* to pick up at a rest stop.

Or *Aftyn* chose, but it doesn't really matter.

I didn't try to catch Aftyn's attention. He came to me. He pulled me off the sidewalk and insisted I ride with them, and while I'd hoped there'd be some benefit to it, that was clearly just some petulant move on his part to try and make Willa jealous for his dick. The guy has one hell of a smile, and a nice body from what I've seen... but I'm not getting the feeling he wants to fuck me with Willa around, and that bitch isn't going anywhere.

That's why I got out of the car.

Not just because I've needed to pee for at least six hours, but because I don't plan on leaving with them.

I've had a rule since the first time a car ride went bad that I never get in the same car twice. If I get out, for any reason, it's a sign that I need to move on. Pick another sucker, find another mode of transportation, and move on. I've only held on this long because I really thought these two might be entertaining, that they might have something redeeming about them to alleviate the constant boredom of life.

Unfortunately, it seems I was wrong.

Once I dug past the curious dynamic of their friendship and poked at the absence of their previous road trip partner, there just wasn't much left to do but pretend to sleep in the backseat and see how far I could get in their car. Missouri is farther West than I've ever been, so that's one accomplishment, and for a kid that was told she would never get out of Chicago—I think I've done pretty well for myself.

The wind whispers through the trees rising high above me, and I like the way the leaves clatter together in a shushing sound, as if the entire forest wants everyone to stay quiet. *Shh, shh, shh...* I used to dread that sound, as far as I can feel much of anything anyway. Not that I was ever really afraid when Brian started coming to my room instead of Lauren's, but I just didn't want to deal with it. The walls in that fucking foster home were so thin that I'd known what he was doing to her for months. I could hear him talking, hear the bed moving, hear her crying—which is probably why he changed his mind and picked me.

He used to say my silence was creepy. That I weirded him out with the way I watched him and everyone else. It was his favorite topic of conversation whenever he started drinking, but apparently, I wasn't too creepy to fuck. Suddenly my quiet was a benefit. *His* benefit. But, once Brian started using my body at night, he didn't say a word against me, and I liked not having to deal with his shit during the daylight hours. He chose another one of the kids to be his verbal punching bag, or his idiot of a wife, and he never really talked to me when he showed up and climbed in my bed. Just the occasional groan, the occasional comment about how good I felt, the rhetorical questions on whether or not I liked it. I ignored all of it, but for some reason I couldn't block out the sound of him shushing me whenever I made the slightest sound. He'd put his hand over my mouth, his lips right by my ear, and hiss out each goddamn syllable.

Shh, shh, shh...

Fucking pedophile.

Lauren was fifteen when he started with her, at least she *looked* older—but I was twelve. He had no excuse, and after four years of that shit I finally decided to get out of there and see if the rest of the world was as tedious and miserable as that house in Chicago.

Brian never saw the knife I'd taken from the kitchen, and I made sure to go for the neck so he wouldn't make too much noise. As I knelt down beside him, meeting his gaze in the dim glow of the streetlights coming through my window, I was completely mesmerized. The sheer surprise in his eyes, the way his mouth opened and closed, the choking sounds coming from the hole in his throat. It was the first time I'd ever felt alive... watching him die. But before the light went out in his eyes, I put my fingers over his lips and whispered, '*Shh, shh, shh.*'

I don't know if he got the joke, or if there was enough blood getting to his brain to actually recognize the creativity of me using his own words against him— but I guess I'll never know. Dead people aren't exactly talkative, and I didn't have time to linger anyway.

I'd already packed a bag, using the nice backpack Brian got the time he decided he wanted to be 'outdoorsy,' Although, where he expected to do that in Chicago, I have no fucking idea. It's a good backpack though, it's lasted me all this time, and I'd filled it earlier that day with everything I needed to walk out the door. Adding the knife I'd used on him felt like the final piece.

Well, technically not the *final* piece. That was probably the two containers of gasoline I poured over the living room and around the front and back doors. My last goodbye to that foster home was the strike of a match and the quiet close of a door.

It's impressive how fast fire can spread when there's an accelerant involved, and when I stopped down the street to watch beside someone's truck, I felt a real smile when I first saw the smoke, the flickering light in the windows. I've looked it up at a few public libraries in the year or so since I walked away from there, and gasoline is one of the most common accelerants used in arson.

It was a disappointing thing to learn. To realize I'd done something so... average.

But, it's fine. I'm not a firebug. I didn't get tingly in my pants watching the fire eat the house and the rest of the idiots inside. It wasn't even fun watching people leave their houses in a panic, and I didn't stick around long enough to catch the attention of the fire department or the police.

No, the only thing that made me feel alive was watching Brian die, and that knife was the first one I added to my collection.

When I started hitchhiking, I used to think about him a lot. Wondering if killing someone who hadn't been such an asshole to me would feel different. Could it possibly feel better? Would it feel the same? Or would it just be... boring. Like everything else.

Fortunately, the world outside of Chicago is full of people just like Brian. I wasn't on the road long before I got the chance to test my theories. When the asshole made it clear what he expected for the ride in his car, all it took was letting him have his fun the first time he made a move, not fighting or making a sound, just like with Brian—and then it was easy to slice him open while he slept.

I used to remember his name, but I don't anymore. I just remember the way his intestines spilled out of the hole in his skin like some kind of weird jack-in-the-box made by an evil clown while he desperately tried to put them back.

The bad news was that I killed him in the car, which smelled pretty terrible even after I rolled his body into a ditch.

The good news was that I felt more real watching him take his last breath than I had with Brian. I think it was the lighting.

So much easier to see with the sun out.

Still, not every ride is a bad one. Sometimes people feed me, give me money, rent me a room at a motel that they don't plan on sharing with me. I'm sure if I wasn't pretty, and if I didn't play the lost little girl, I'd get a lot less of the nice kind of help. But those rides are good. Easy. I let those people live as my version of a thank you—even if they don't understand just how gracious I've been. The bad rides all end the same, but at least I get a vehicle that I can drive until it runs out of gas, along with whatever cash or useful shit they've got in it.

Riding with Aftyn and Willa hasn't been good, but it hasn't been bad either. It's just been... boring.

There was so much potential for them to be interesting, for us to have fun one way or another, but they're too caught up in whatever bullshit they've got going on between them. Friends, not friends. Lovers, not lovers. It's like some terrible sitcom that I was the single unwilling audience member for.

Time to unsubscribe.

Sighing, I stumble upon a trail and follow it until I touch road again. It's narrow, black, and looks similar to where Willa parked her car, but I've been walking for a while so even if it is... they're nowhere nearby. Walking along the edge of it, I eventually see a campground sign pointing to the left and I head toward it. Campground might mean people camping, which could mean food, and although I'm pretty good at ignoring the twist of hunger in my belly, I'm also not stupid enough to pass up a chance to find someone else who might let me hitch a ride—and feed me in the meantime.

There's a dark blue SUV parked all by itself at the head of a trail that promises camping sites near the lake. Crossing my fingers that they're here to camp and not just hike around, I move down the path until I see a bright green tent through the trees. I'm already warming up my 'vulnerable and helpless' voice when I realize their campsite is empty. No voices, no fire going. Risking a peek into their tent, I can't believe my luck when I see plastic bags of food and a pair of duffel bags.

"Let's see what you've got for me," I mumble and drop my backpack. Digging through their shit, I find some clothes in the girl's bag that might fit me, and some protein bars and snacks to shove in my pack. The gallon jug of water is tempting, but I don't want to carry it. So, I just refill my water bottle and sit down on the ground to drink my fill, eating a couple of protein bars while I listen to the trees and keep my ears open for the return of these idiots.

Ten minutes later—nada.

Huffing, I put their shit back together, zipping their duffels shut so they won't know I messed with it if I can find them, and then I close up their tent and head toward the lake. Just as I come over a rise, I see them, and my skin prickles, goose bumps rising on my arms as I see two people lying near the water. And, well... they're definitely not sleeping. No one really lays face down in the mud, or face up in it with their torso shredded and their pale limbs smeared with red.

There's a reason red is my favorite color, and *this* is why. It just looks so pretty in every shade. The paler streaks of it on his arms, the dull red where it's stained his clothes, and then that deep, almost black hue where it's pooled in the holes on his stomach.

I'm so distracted by the sight of the two, that it takes me longer than it really should to connect the dots—or, rather, to connect the blood spatter.

We've been out here for a while now, and I haven't heard another vehicle. As far as I know the only people in this area of the forest are me, these two dead fucks, and the unfriendly not-lovers. Grinning, I look over at the knife on the ground and decide I should add it to my collection.

A keepsake.

But when I bend down to pick it up, I see

something even better amidst the blood-stained dirt and leaves. A little glint that turns out to be a ring. The same ring that was on Willa's hand when she reached back for her phone.

Maybe they're more fun than I thought.

Grabbing the ring and the knife, I head to the edge of the water to rinse them both off. Once I'm sure the blood is gone, I slip them into my backpack and head back in the direction of their SUV at a jog.

Sure, I almost never get in the same car twice, but that's mostly because people get very boring after a while. People tend to show their true colors faster than anyone would care to admit aloud and it's almost always disappointing. Aftyn and Willa, though? They're just starting to get really interesting.

And I should probably return her ring at some point as a thank you for the ride. It would be the nice thing to do... if I can make it back before they leave me behind anyway.

When Willa's shiny SUV appears around a curve in the road, I almost choke on a laugh, but I swallow it down and focus on breathing evenly. They're not back and, judging by the scene they left behind, I'm pretty sure they're washing off in the lake.

Hell, it's worth getting back in the car just to see how they explain away any blood stains on their clothes.

I climb back into my spot in the backseat, getting comfortable against the door so I can focus on slowing my heart rate and my breathing so I can pretend to be asleep. But it's hard because I actually feel... excited? I think that's what this is.

There's just so many options for how this could turn out. So many potential outcomes, both thrilling and disastrous.

But one thing's for sure. I'm definitely not bored.

Best. Hitchhike. Ever.

TWENTY-FIVE

Silence is Golden

THE AGITATOR

I smile when the lights in the theater finally dim. After all the previews I was forced to sit through, the opening credits begin to set the tone of the movie, and I finally lean back in my seat to get comfortable. The crescendo that blares over the large Dolby digital speakers housed in the four corners, as well as those strategically placed in the center walls of the somewhat packed theater, sends a rush through me.

I haven't really been out to enjoy life in what seems like forever, so tonight is a treat.

I have a bucket of popcorn in my hand, a drink in my cupholder, and a small mountain of napkins balanced on my thigh.

I'm happy.

It's such a strange feeling, but I am.

Until the back of my seat gets kicked and the

bucket jostles hard enough in my hands to spill some of my popcorn.

Ignore the children, I tell myself.

I take a deep breath and decide it was an accident. I won't let something so miniscule ruin my night out, especially not when I worked so hard for the money that I decided to treat myself with.

Clearing my throat, I reach into my popcorn and pull out another handful, nibbling at each piece as the scene before me unfolds.

The typical stormy night, a girl running from someone that's chasing her, and a flash of lightning to tell us where the bad guy is.

If only life were that simple.

A wry smile creases my lips as I reach for my drink to wash down the taste of butter in my mouth.

Then it happens.

Something that I know is going to get me into a lot of trouble with almost everyone in the theater if I can't control it and fast.

Buzz, buzz, buzz...

"Who the fuck has their phone on?" the person in the row behind barks at the top of his lungs.

I push down the bottom part of the seat next to me and set my bucket of popcorn in it, hoping that it won't close against it and ruin my night by destroying my treat. Once I'm sure it's okay, I do my best to slide my hand inconspicuously into my jacket pocket. I begin to brush my fingers against any and all buttons hoping that it will get it to stop.

And for a moment, it does.

Swallowing a sigh of relief, I reach for my bucket of popcorn, when...

Buzz, buzz, buzz...

This can't be happening, I think unhappily.

"Turn off that fucking phone!" the patron behind me barks.

A round of nervous giggles and some muttered agreements echo throughout the theater.

I quickly reach for some of the napkins on my leg before I shove the rest into the empty cupholder on the other side of me, then get to my feet and walk out of the theater.

I can only hope that there's some other idiot in there that forgot to turn off their phone too so that I'm not giving myself up.

Once in the lobby, I glance around until I see the signs for the restrooms, then practically run inside.

I walk down the line of stalls until I settle on the one in the middle, step in, then close the door behind me.

Buzz, buzz, buzz...

I pull the phone out of my pocket and shake my head, a rueful smile dancing on my lips.

Persistent little fucker.

I sit down on the toilet seat as I send the call to

voicemail. I'm not ready to talk to him just yet but I know he won't stop until he hears my voice.

But that would ruin the game, wouldn't it?

I roll my neck from left to right and back again, ready to turn off my phone and go back and catch the rest of the movie. I'm hoping I haven't missed any important plot points, or I'll end up having to rent the damn thing on DVD when it comes out.

Getting to my feet, phone still in hand and my finger on the power button, I smile when a message comes through at just the right moment.

Give me the fucking address. The right one. I'm almost there.

I quickly tap the information that's been so kindly asked of me before I shut the phone off and walk over to the sink to wash my hands.

Hopefully, this was the right thing to do.

TWENTY-SIX

The Road to Hell is Paved with Betrayal

WILLA

The bitch is still in the car when Aftyn and I finally come back. On top of everything else that's happened today, I was really hoping that the universe would cut me a fucking break and have made her disappear. Either off to be someone else's problem, or off a cliff—I really don't give a shit. I just didn't want to have to deal with her on top of Aftyn.

He killed Dexter.

It was my first instinct, the first thought that showed up in my head when he came back from the bathrooms with that whore on his arm and Dexter nowhere in sight... but I'd hoped. I'd hoped he wouldn't kill him because he knew that Dexter was my friend, that I cared about him. Hell, why else would I have always made sure the kid had food?

But Aftyn doesn't give a shit about any of that.

He never liked Dexter, never liked how much time I spent with him or how I took care of someone *other* than him. If the world isn't revolving around Aftyn, he'll move heaven and earth to rearrange things so it is. The fucking son of a bitch.

"Get in the car, Wills." Aftyn is holding open the passenger door and it hurts me to even look at him. Every time I look at his fucking face, I just see Dexter.

Refusing to respond, I get in the car and put on the seat belt as he slams the door shut a lot harder than necessary. I can hear Daphne waking up in the backseat, but I don't have the energy to even make a comment about how she didn't disappear when we gave her the chance. Hugging my purse in my lap, I turn toward the window, clenching my jaw hard when Aftyn starts fucking whistling as he gets in the driver's side.

"I need the keys, Wills." He taps my arm and I slap his hand away before digging out the keys and dangling them from my finger toward him. Aftyn doesn't just take the keys though, he grabs my forearm and yanks me toward him, fingers digging into my skin painfully hard. "Look at me."

I don't do it right away. I keep my gaze defiantly focused on the steering wheel, but eventually he starts tightening his hold, hard enough to leave bruises, and I lift my eyes to glare at him. I know he sees the rage I've still got burning like a forest fire under the surface. He saw it explode. Letting that rage out is exhausting though, and I still don't know why I turned it on that random couple instead of him. He betrayed me. He lied to me. He took my friend from me. And even when I was holding a goddamn knife... I didn't go for him.

I just cried. *Pathetic.*

The only reason I'm not shoving my fucking thumbs into his eye sockets right now is because my arms are jelly. I spent all my energy bashing that bitch's head on a rock and stabbing her boytoy a million times. But even when Aftyn smirks, I know he's thinking about me killing them. I'm sure he thinks he can take me, but this rage isn't going anywhere, I just need time to refresh my energy stores before I get some revenge.

"Going to behave while I drive?" he asks, tilting his head, that cocky smirk stretching a little. "I could always try out some bondage if you're still feeling feisty."

I don't respond, I just drop my eyes and yank my arm out of his grasp. Aftyn laughs under his breath and snags the keys, cranking the car as I curl up against the door again. As soon as we've got power, I roll up my window while he rolls his down. The flick of a lighter grates on my nerves further, but he's smoked so many cigarettes in my fucking car at this point that it just doesn't matter anymore. He'll pay for the detail whenever we get home. *If* we both get back home.

At this point I'm not sure if anyone in the car is going to make it out of this alive, because there's still a chance I'll turn my rage on Daphne before I take it out on Aftyn. It's my goddamn pity for him rearing its head again, but he doesn't deserve it anymore. Not after this. I just have to figure out how to stop caring about him.

A couple of hours later, Aftyn is back to whistling between drags on his cigarette as we speed down the highway at least fifteen miles over the speed limit. If I were speaking to him right now, I'd tell him to slow the fuck down, because if he gets a ticket *I* will be the one that ends up having to pay it.

But it's not worth breaking the silent treatment I've got going with him right now.

He's tried to bait me into conversation a few different times, and he's even talked to Daphne about me just trying to get me to speak—but I'm not going to give him the satisfaction. If I have to feel this miserable, I want everyone in the car to feel it too.

And I am miserable. Heartbroken. Devastated.

I should have known better than to try and get Aftyn to look twice at Dex. If this is anyone's fault... it's mine. I just wanted to make Dex happy, to see him happy for one fucking day of his life, and Aftyn could have given him that so easily. It wouldn't have taken much. I'm not talking about making out with Dex, or letting him blow him, but just being slightly less of an asshole would have been enough. Instead, he complained every time Dexter hung out with us. Loudly. He mocked him right to his face, and Dex is —*was*—sensitive. He was never like me or Aftyn, he couldn't fight back verbally or physically, and without the ability to be an utter asshole... he never stood a chance against Aftyn.

And Aftyn knew it.

He saw every weakness in Dexter and exploited them. Taunted him with them, teased him with the possibility of affection only to laugh in his face, when he reacted with the slightest bit of hope. I never really found out what led Dexter to the rough life he led, or why he never had enough money for food or decent clothes. I never wanted to press him, because I wanted him to let me help him. I wanted him to feel like someone on the planet gave a shit about him.

Instead, I served him up on a silver platter to Aftyn.

I let him walk away from me, away from my ability to protect him, even though I had that sick feeling in my stomach as I watched them walk toward the bathrooms together. My last act in Dexter's life was *not* acting. Not speaking up, not standing up to Aftyn, not doing anything at all. And he died in a fucking bathroom stall.

The urge to cry again makes me bite down on my tongue, and I almost bite right through it when I hear Daphne speak up from the backseat.

"Are you guys hungry?"

I'm tempted to tell her to shut the fuck up, but Aftyn's heavy sigh keeps me quiet. He glances up at the rearview mirror, his expression flat as he responds to her in a bored tone. "You're still here?"

"Um, yes?" she replies in her stupid soft voice, which I'm pretty fucking confident isn't her real voice. Everything about this girl is fake, and all I can hope is that Aftyn has finally seen through her shit as he rolls his eyes.

"Well, I'm not stopping. We're making good time right now."

"Okay." Daphne doesn't say anything else, and even though I'm still pissed at him, I feel a smile tugging at my lips. Turning farther toward the window, I hide it, because I don't want him to know that his bullshit is still able to entertain me.

Maybe if I wait long enough Aftyn will finally finish toying with her and he'll take her out for me. I'd like to see that, especially since it's so obvious she wants his dick. *Everyone* wants Aftyn, but despite the occasional drunken make-out session, I've refused to cross that line with him. If he fucks her, I don't know how I'll feel about it. I definitely don't want to watch that part, but I'd like to see him kill her. To watch her hope die in the same way that I'm sure Dexter's did. It's only fair since she took his space in the backseat that she should suffer like he did—*worse* than he did.

Not that I plan on asking Aftyn the details of what he did to Dex.

As the car falls silent again, the subtle rumble of the road calms me and before I know it the exhaustion is creeping in and I'm asleep.

"*One way or another I'm gonna find ya, I'm gonna get ya get ya get ya get ya*!" The radio blares to life and I jerk awake, glaring at Aftyn as he quickly flips through the stations, trying to find something to listen to, but he hasn't turned the volume down at all.

Groaning, I sit up straight, working out the ache in my neck from sleeping hunched against the door. There's absolutely fucking nothing out the window. Just open plains, and I don't understand why anyone would choose to live in this part of the country. It's just... ugly. Flat and brown. When there are so many pretty places in the US, it seems stupid to live here. Wherever the fuck we are.

Aftyn settles on some station playing random songs from the 90s and 2000s, and I reach over to turn down the volume but he slaps my hand. "Driver picks the music, Wills. Hands off."

"Then pull the fuck over and I'll drive."

"Why don't you go back to moping while I focus on getting us there?" Aftyn sneers and my rage floods back like he reached in and flipped a switch in my head.

Before I can even think about what I'm doing, I'm punching his arm and trying to slap him. I feel the car swerve, but all I want to do is hurt him. I want him to feel how I feel on the inside. Like he's carved out a piece of me and tossed it away.

"STOP. THE. FUCKING. CAR." I shout at him between strikes, most of which aren't doing much of anything except putting our lives in danger, but eventually he gets a hand on my shoulder and shoves me hard into the window. My head bounces off it but I don't even feel the ache, and I'm about to launch myself at him again when I realized he's laughing. Hard. He gasps in breath to let out another laugh, holding his hand out toward me.

"Fuck, okay. Okay, Wills. Chill. I'll pull over at that rest stop ahead." Chuckling, Aftyn sweeps his hand back through his hair, glancing at himself in the mirror. The side of his face is a little pink near his temple, and I may have given him a few bruises on his arm, but it's nowhere near enough. Our positions in the car made it too awkward to really get a good swing in, but at least he knows I'm not fucking around anymore.

Crossing my arms, I press myself back into the seat and wait for him to take the exit, bringing us to the parking lot. Just the sight of the rest area makes my stomach clench, and I throw my car door open the second he slides the shifter into park. "Get out!"

"You gotta calm down, Wills." Aftyn is still grinning

and laughing under his breath like me wanting to rip his goddamn head off is hilarious. When I yank the driver's side door open, it takes all my self-control not to punch him right in the nose. The way he's smirking at me I can tell he's waiting for it, and I know he can hurt me a lot more than I can hurt him in an even fight.

"Out," I growl through clenched teeth, and he unbuckles his seat belt, raising his hands up as he drops to the ground.

"You know... if you put on some leather, carried a whip, I might really be into this." Aftyn winks at me, and I shove past him to get in the car, but he's leaning on the damn door when I turn around to shut it—and he's not smiling anymore. "But, unless you plan on spanking me before you suck my dick and bend over for me, you need to stop bossing me around. Got it?"

I'm still so angry that I'm tempted to tell him to go to hell, or launch myself at him and beat his head against the asphalt. But that's what he wants. He wants me to go after him so he can show me that he's in charge, and he definitely fucking isn't. Turning away from him, I start the car and look back at Daphne. She's got a slight smile on her face and I want to slap it off her more than anything in the world. Instead, I just smile back. "Get out of my fucking car."

"What?" Her eyes widen a little and I point toward the door.

"Get. Out. Of. My. Fucking. Car." I enunciate each word clearly and she looks past me at Aftyn. "Don't look at him! I'm driving now and I want you out of my goddamn car."

"Why don't you make her get out of the car, Willa?" Aftyn has leaned too close to me, speaking right against the shell of my ear, and I can feel the heat of his breath on his next exhale. "Show her what you're made of."

Bringing my elbow back hard, I'm surprised when I actually catch him in the ribs, and he starts laughing as he backs off.

"Your choice, Wills. But if you don't have the ovaries to kick her out yourself, then I think she's going to hang around a little longer." Grinning, Aftyn walks as slow as fucking possible around the front of the SUV, and I'm so tempted to run him over, or drive off without him. Leave him in the same kind of miserable, roadside hole he left Dexter in—but then I'd still be stuck with Daphne, and halfway across the US for no goddamn reason.

So, I just slam the door and grip the steering wheel until my knuckles turn white.

Aftyn is taking his sweet time, stretching his back out beside the car, and I don't think I've ever wanted to hurt him this much. He always pisses me off, he likes to push my buttons, but killing Dexter was too far and he knows it. When he finally gets in, I give him the same courtesy he gave me when we left Dexter behind— absolutely none. I throw the SUV into drive and speed out of the parking lot before he even has his door shut.

Unfortunately, all Aftyn does is chuckle under his breath, as he adjusts himself in the seat and buckles up. Reaching in front of my face, he plucks his pack of cigarettes from the visor, and I just grit my teeth as I listen to him light up, cracking his window when we hit the highway again. I want him to suffer, and the only way I can think of doing it right now is by letting Daphne in on his stupid fucking secret.

"Hey Daphne, since you're apparently following us around like a bad case of herpes, why don't you ask Aftyn about why we're going to Arizona?" I glance up at her in the rear-view and she meets my eyes for a moment before she stares at the back of the headrest in front of her. I can see Aftyn's jaw muscle twitching, and I smile as I turn to face the highway again.

It takes a minute for Daphne to build up the courage, but she finally breaks the quiet. "Why are you going to Arizona?"

"None of your business."

"He's going to meet his daddy for the first time," I answer her, smiling at Aftyn when he glares at me with a flash of rage. "His mom was a bitch, but she's been gone a while now. She hated Aftyn because he looked so much like his dad, and now that I've seen a picture?" I blow out a breath, laughing as I see Aftyn's face flushing red with anger. "It's kind of weird how similar they look. Why don't you show her, Aftyn?"

"You're going to pay for that, Willa," he threatens me, and I do exactly what he always does to me when he gets under my skin. I just smile and show him that he doesn't scare me at all.

If we're keeping count, I'm ahead of him on this trip. Two bodies to one. And it's not like Dex would have hurt Aftyn, or fought back. He was in love with him.

"Does your dad know you're coming?" Daphne asks, and for the first time since the bitch showed up, I'm actually glad she's here. At least she's finally being useful.

Aftyn turns around in his seat to stare at her. "Hey, since you seem so keen on using that fucking hole in your face right now, and Willa's busy being a raging bitch, why don't I slide back there and let you suck me off?"

"Um..." Daphne stutters, and I think it's cute that she might actually be flustered by Aftyn's caustic bullshit. I'm so used to his comments that I mostly ignore them, but I'm pretty sure he's serious about the blowjob. It's all he's wanted out of her on this ride anyway.

"Is that a no?" Aftyn asks, sneering at her. "Then shut the fuck up."

An awkward silence falls over the car, but it's only awkward for Daphne and Aftyn so I really don't give a shit. I just push the speed limit, hovering between five and ten miles over as I follow the highway signs toward Texas. I didn't even realize we'd arrived in Oklahoma, which means we're finally over the halfway mark on this nightmare road trip.

Hopefully now that I've baited Aftyn, he'll do something about Daphne sooner rather than later. I'm done with her, done with listening to his shit and his threats. He likes to pretend we're best friends, but I've always treated him better than he's ever treated me. I've been a better friend every step of the way.

Eventually I fill the silence with a decent radio station, keeping the volume at a more reasonable level. Both Daphne and Aftyn are leaned against the passenger side of the car, and I don't know if they're trying to sleep or just trying to avoid interacting, but it doesn't matter. I appreciate the peace and quiet and the absence of any of Aftyn's bullshit or Daphne's annoyingly fake voice.

Letting the simmering anger fuel the drive makes the hours pass by fast, and I realize that the only benefit of this much flat land is that the sunset is pretty fantastic. It paints the clouds in a wild array of pinks and oranges, catching the sky on fire as we chase the sunset.

Of course, the sun wins.

As night covers the car, I finally start to feel tired, and hungry. The bitch asked about food a while ago, but I haven't seen much of anything resembling actual civilization since before we even crossed the border into Texas. It's just a lot of flat, open land, and that's a lot less interesting when you can't see anything but what the headlights illuminate. When signs start popping up for Amarillo, I focus on getting there and finding a decent place to fill up on gas and grab something to eat.

Even driving eighty on the empty highway, it still takes almost an hour to reach the outer edges of Amarillo—but it takes longer than that for me to find a place I'm actually willing to stop my car. Everything here looks cheap, and I miss New York even more as I finally pull into a newer looking gas station.

"Um, Willa? Are you getting snacks?" Daphne asks and I take a deep breath so that I don't start screaming at her around complete strangers.

"Yes."

"Can you get me some stuff?"

Turning to look at her, I'm about to ask her why she thinks I'd buy her anything, but then I see a little wallet in her hands and I realize she actually *does* have cash. Rolling my eyes, I hold out my hand and take the wad of bills from her. "Fine. But you'll be happy with whatever the fuck I get."

"Yeah, sure." Daphne nods, smiling at me, and I ignore her, looking at Aftyn instead. He's got his phone in his hands, and then he looks up at me and raises an eyebrow.

"What, Willa?"

"Stop being an asshole and fill the car up while I'm inside." I slam the door on whatever bullshit Aftyn tries to say to me and head inside with Daphne's money in my pocket. I just want this trip to be over already, even though I have no idea what life is going to be like when we finally get back home.

It doesn't seem like anything will feel normal again after this.

Coordinates Received

AFTYN

I'm leaning against Willa's truck, watching the meter run up the dollar signs. It amazes me that this thing takes so much fucking gas, but that means no more stops.

Once we're back on the road, it's straight to Lakyn's place.

With a sigh, I fish my phone out of my pocket and pull up the message that my goddamn phantom sent with an address. Regardless of what Willa says, I'll take over the driving from here.

I brush the tip of my finger along the address, copy it, and paste it into the navigation system app on my phone. I want to make sure that this isn't some kind of—

Motherfucker, I growl internally.

I tap the screen and bring up the Earthy view of the

map, grinding my teeth when I see that the address I received is to some burned out house. I highly doubt that Lakyn would live in such a shithole. Even though I don't really know him at all, I have a feeling that he has more taste than that.

I look up at the meter when the pump makes a *click* sound. I squeeze the last few cents into the tank before I pull it out and replace it.

Turning my eyes toward the small *Smart Shop* a few feet away, I can see Willa in line. She's watching me through narrowed eyes, and I know that it's only a matter of time before she really does gun for my balls.

Bitch.

I lean into the truck and take the keys out of the ignition so that leaving me behind doesn't become an option. If I had to walk to Arizona from here, I'd get there looking like shit and he'd probably laugh me out of the state.

I want to make an impression on him.

I can't explain it, but I just want him to see me differently than Mom ever did.

I blow my breath out, impatiently waiting for Wills. I don't want to leave Daphne alone with her, but I'd rather not leave her precious fucking truck unattended either.

While Daphne may be inside of it, that girl's mind is as occupied as one's can get.

As soon as I see Wills making her way out of the

store looking as angry as when she first went in, I walk away from the truck, brush by her roughly, and go sit on the side of the building. I run a hand back through my hair, wondering if I should just try calling again, but I just have a feeling that this won't go my way.

I decide against it.

If my tormentor doesn't answer the phone, it'll put me in a really bad fucking mood and that'll sour the rest of the trip for me.

I begin to chew the inside of my mouth as I pull up the navigation app and screenshot the information I located with the bogus address, then go to my messages. I tap on the phone number, attach the picture, and send it along with a little love note.

If you don't give me the right fucking address, I'll come looking for you instead of Lakyn. Think you can take me?

Closing my eyes, I lean my head back against the building and wait. I don't always get a response as soon as I send a heartwarming message, but whoever this is has to know how close I am right now.

Or maybe they think I'm fucking around and am still sitting in Tribeca somewhere—who the fuck knows?

Ding!

I almost drop my phone when the notification goes off.

I glance down and swipe the message open, my eyes narrowing at a new address.

Catch me if you can.

I'm going to kill whoever the fuck this is. Maybe that'll be a good way to impress my old man, maybe it won't be, but this son of a bitch is playing games with the wrong guy.

I run my finger over the address, drop it into my navigation app and wait while it spins for a moment, and then I see it.

A house I don't know in a street I'm unfamiliar with.

And inside?

The man that gave me life and hasn't thought about me since.

I get to my feet and walk back to the truck only to find Wills standing by the open driver's side door.

"I'm driving," I tell her, giving her a rough shove to the side.

I'm not in the mood for a game of whose dick is bigger than whose. I have my fucking destination now after God knows how many hours stuck in a truck with a bitch that hates me and another one that doesn't even seem to know what fucking planet she's on—now it's my turn to finally get something good in my life and I'm not giving up driving so she can take her sweet ass time and make this longer than it needs to be.

Willa narrows her eyes at me, runs a finger along her neck to let me know that she's still got her mind set to kill and I roll my eyes.

If she wants to fucking scuffle, I'll engage her.

After we've left Arizona.

Over four hours due west and we cross into New Mexico somewhere between quiet sobs and raging thoughts.

While I know that the third wheel in the back seat is probably asleep again, I can't help but wonder how far she thinks I'm going to take her.

There's no way in hell I want her to meet my father—Hell, it wasn't even any of her business why we were taking this long, miserable road trip to begin with.

But you just had to open your mouth and flap those gums, I think testily as I steal a glance at Willa.

She's pressed against the window again, and I can't help but wish the goddamn door would give way and she'd go tumbling out onto the gravel.

Normally, we'd be able to talk shit out, but I know that our friendship can't be saved now, and to be quite honest, I'm not entirely sure I care anymore.

Now she knows how I really feel about her and she'll either deal with it or fuck off out of my life.

I run a hand irritably over my face before I rest my elbow on the window frame. Even so, I wish things could be different between us.

We make a hell of a team when we're on the same

side, but it's rare that we see eye to eye on shit these days.

And that was before I left her conscience in a dirty rest area bathroom stall.

She should have known better.

I told her over and over again that I wasn't interested in Dexter. I've never even been remotely curious about switching teams, yet she persisted.

'Just give him a chance, Aftyn! Even if you don't want to fuck him, be nice to him once in a while! He really is a great guy!'

I know how shit works, though.

You spend too much time being nice to the wrong person and they always stab you in the back. That's why I've always preferred Wills—at least she stabs me in the front.

Damn near fifteen minutes alone with my thoughts, I glance up and smile slightly when I see a sign for Albuquerque. I think that's where that church is that she wanted to check out, so I do the one thing I can't stand.

I swallow my fucking pride and point it out.

"Hey," I say, reaching over and giving her thigh a nudge. She immediately smacks my hand away and shoots a dirty look at me, but I do my best to maintain my composure while I have her attention and nod toward the sign.

Albuquerque, I-40 W.

"Wanna check it out?" I ask her.

"What I want," she begins, her tone already dripping with venom, "is to fucking get this over with so I can ditch your ass when we get back home."

I let out a heavy sigh as I roll my eyes at the road in front of me and press down on the gas pedal.

Whatever the fuck Lakyn turns out to be like, he can't be worse than this.

TWENTY-EIGHT

The Masks We Wear

DAPHNE

Completely dysfunctional.

That's how I describe Aftyn, Willa, and their relationship. I'm not sure how these two met, but clearly they should have kept on going. The fact that they circle each other like a pair of wolves vying for the alpha spot in a pack of two just proves it. Constantly snapping and biting at each other, but neither of them willing to actually go for the throat and make a fucking move.

Instead, they turned their proverbial teeth on the couple back in the forest, which was apparently not as fun as it looked.

Willa's been furious since she got back in the car, and then she completely lost it on the highway when Aftyn blasted the radio. It was meant to piss her off, but I think it worked better than Aftyn expected. I hadn't seen her lose her shit like that yet, but it's nice to know she has it in her—and I've been learning so many things about them since I decided to get back in their car.

Aftyn has daddy issues. Mommy is gone.

And Willa is a hell of a lot more volatile than she looks. It was her bloody ring I found by the guy stabbed into oblivion, and the way she went after Aftyn when he wouldn't pull over to let her drive was the kind of snap, crackle, crazy that I just wouldn't expect from the pretty, petite blonde. She really seems more like the start-a-mean-rumor type than the stab-you-a-hundred-times type, but that's one thing that makes life worth living. Finding those people who are so much more than they seem.

I still don't like her, and she's definitely a conniving little snake, but I can respect another girl who uses her looks to trick everyone around her into thinking she's harmless.

Still, their silence is irritating. I want them to argue again, or get into an actual fight, not just silent treatment each other as we continue on through New Mexico past whatever giant ball o' twine Aftyn offered to show her. I get that they're on their way to meet Aftyn's real dad, but they could have flown a hell of a lot faster. One thing is clear, these two should have never been crammed in a car together for an extended road trip.

Although, I can't help but stifle a laugh as I think about the sheer probability of three killers ending up in the same car together. Them through whatever strange twist of fate bound them, and me by sheer chance.

What are the odds?

The more I think about it, the more funny it becomes. I know they're both annoyed by my presence at this point because I'm crowding their little pissing contest by just existing in the backseat, but I'm actually curious how they'd react if they knew my secret.

"Fucking finally," Aftyn mutters, and I look out the window to see a sign welcoming us to Arizona. Willa sits up straight in the front seat, and I lean over to look at the map on Aftyn's phone. We're actually getting close, and that means I don't have much time left to have some fun with them.

"Hey, Willa?" I unzip my backpack, digging inside it carefully as I hear her heavy sigh.

"Don't talk to me."

"Um, okay..." I feel my smile stretch as I pull out her ring and stare at it for a moment before I hold it up. "I just thought you might like your ring back."

"What?" she snaps, twisting around in the seat to stare at the little shiny circle for a moment before she sneers and grabs it. "You fucking pickpocket! What, did you take this off me while I was sleeping?"

"Actually, I found it back in the forest by—"

"This bitch is a fucking thief, Aftyn," Willa snarls, finally speaking to her counterpart again. "I don't know why the hell you picked her up, but you need to just finish whatever you've got planned and get rid of her."

"Stop telling me what to do, Willa." His tone is low, dark, and his grip on the steering wheel is just a little too tight.

"What's the plan then?" she snaps, waving a hand at me in the backseat as I fiddle with the knife I picked up at the same time as her ring. "Either you're going to fuck her, immediately get bored, and drop her on the side of the road, or you're going to kill her like you killed Dexter. I don't give a fuck which one, just do it already!"

Aftyn killed Dexter? Interesting.

"Right now I want to leave both of you by the side of the goddamn road!" Aftyn shouts. Clenching his jaw, he yanks the cigarettes from the visor and bites the end of one to take it out of the pack. A second later he's lighting it and putting the pack away again while Willa fumes in the passenger seat.

"Jesus Christ, just find a place to pull off and I'll do it. There's gotta be some empty place around here," Willa says, and I decide that the direct death threat is just a little too far for the pretty little princess.

Pulling the knife they used on the guy from my bag, I lean forward and reach over the back of the passenger seat to quickly grab a fistful of her hair in my left hand, placing the blade against her throat with my right. "Oh, Willa... didn't your mother ever teach you not to pick up hitchhikers?"

When she lets out a little gasp and goes completely still, I get that tingly rush in my skin that feels like being truly alive. It's like the world gets color in it again, and I'm itching to pull the knife back and slice her throat open... but not yet.

"Are you fucking kidding me?" Aftyn groans, a cloud of smoke swirling in and out of the car before the window finally sucks it all out, and I let my smile stretch as he doesn't lift a single finger to help the bitch.

"Did you hear me, Willa?"

"Yeah, I fucking heard you," she snaps, and I twist my fist in her hair just to remind her of the situation.

"Well, there's a reason you're not supposed to pick up hitchhikers. You never which ones are dangerous... but you know what's been cracking me up for the last twelve hours?" I ask, letting out the laugh I can feel bubbling up in my chest.

"What?" Willa asks, but her voice is flat, annoyed, and I can tell she doesn't *really* want to know what I've been thinking about. No, she wants to kill me. Unfortunately for her, she's in the front fucking seat and I've got a knife to her goddamn throat, so I get to tell her anyway.

"I've been thinking about the absolute fucking odds of both of you being killers, on this little road trip even though you clearly don't like each other—and then you pick *me* up?" I shake my head a little as I glance over at Aftyn whose eyes are drifting casually between me, Willa, and the road. "I mean, if you were just looking for someone to toy with and kill, you probably ran into a lot of people before you stumbled on me at that rest stop. Unless, Willa's right and you were just looking for an easy fuck, Aftyn?"

He takes a long drag on his cigarette, letting it out in a cloud as he stares straight ahead. "All I want right now is the both of you to shut up so I can get where I'm going."

"Aftyn," Willa growls. "Fucking do something."

"I told you to handle it, Wills, but you were too pissed at me to take my advice." Aftyn flicks his cigarette against the window edge. "She's your problem right now, not mine. All she wants from me is my dick."

"I've got other things on my mind right now, actually," I reply, bringing the blade closer to her throat. "You know, I'm not a very talkative person usually. I like to watch people, wait for them to show me who they really are... but you two seemed so boring and shallow at first. Then I found the little mess you left behind in the woods, and I found your ring beside this pretty blade here, and I actually felt a little excited."

"Why? Did you think we'd suddenly be besties if you told us you've killed someone?" Willa scoffs. "This isn't a fucking secret club, *Daphne*. I don't give a shit if you're Manson's long lost kid, you're still annoying as fuck and Aftyn should have left you in the gutter with the trash where you belong."

"I'm curious... did you think that little rant would hurt my feelings?" I ask, grinning as I listen to how fast she's breathing. Her words are all cocky, but she's scared. "I don't want to be your friend, Willa. Honestly, I don't give a fuck about either of you. You've brought me closer to California, which I've always wanted to see, so I appreciate that, but the only real reason I've stayed in your fucking car is because after I saw what the two of you were capable of... I thought you might actually be interesting."

"Do I have to listen to this?" Willa asks, and then I feel her jerk when the knife nicks her as the SUV bounces over a bump in the road. "You fucking cut me!"

"See, *this* is what I mean. You two have the potential to be so interesting. So much better than the average boring idiot, and instead you have these petty little fights and pissing contests with each other. You're so concerned about how you're perceived by each other, and everyone else, that you haven't even tried to figure out who you're actually capable of becoming."

"Why would I give a fuck what you have to say?" Willa wraps her fingers around my wrist, just below the hand holding the knife, and I laugh.

"If you think holding my wrist is going to stop this knife from slicing your throat open, you've obviously not played with knives very often."

"I think you're a fucking pussy," she snarls. "You want to find out who the badder bitch is? Then don't be the kind of cunt that kills someone when they can't do shit about it. But, you probably never do that, do you? You're opportunistic and you take cheap shots like this bullshit move because you'd never win in a fair fight."

"I know that you're just trying to save your life, Willa..." I whisper, debating over whether or not I should just slice her throat and end it now.

Her argument is disappointingly pathetic. I've never cared about fair fights. That's for sports and other shit like that. Killing people isn't a team sport, even if they like to treat it like one, and there's no referee going to call foul just because I finally put Willa in her place. The only thing holding me back is that we're still on the highway, and a bloody, dead body in the passenger seat might attract some attention.

That, and I'm still not sure how Aftyn will react when I slice Willa open.

It's better to be out of the car for this, and I have to admit I'm a little curious about whether or not she's got the kind of skills to take me out. Lifting the knife away, I let go of her hair and pat her on the head. "I honestly don't give a fuck if you die fairly. Death is death either way, but you know what? I think I would like to see what you're made of... to find out what you're like when you drop the mask."

Willa twists around in the seat, rage burning in her pretty blue eyes. "Oh, I'll show you what I'm made of just before I gut you, you stupid fucking bitch."

Lifting the knife up, I tilt it back and forth. "Name-calling really doesn't bother me either, but if you keep giving me more reasons to kill you, eventually I'm just going to decide that shutting you up is more entertaining than seeing just how interesting you might be before you die."

"Yeah, we'll see who's standing when all is said and done," she grumbles over her shoulder as she drops back into her seat, and I let her have the last word. I'm not playing the same game she and Aftyn are playing. I don't care whether they like me or not, and I definitely don't want to be the alpha of whatever little pack they've formed.

Still, I'm not an idiot. I keep the knife in my hand, resting on my thigh, just in case Willa or Aftyn decide to play *my* game a little early.

Otherwise, I guess we'll just resolve this after Aftyn meets his dad.

TWENTY-NINE

The Devil in the Flesh

AFTYN

The street is quiet when I finally turn onto it.

My hands are shaking, and I can't tell if it's because of these bitches going at each other or if it's because I'm nervous. The latter would be a foreign emotion to me and that's what's fucking with me right now.

Nerves are for the weak and I'm *not* weak.

I grit my teeth as Daphne giggles and Willa turns to glare at her again, but I keep my eyes on the numbers of the houses as they begin to go up. I lower the radio so I can see better and glance at the navigation system.

Five hundred feet on the left.

Swallowing the lump in my throat, I ease off the gas because if I drive past the house, I don't know if I'll turn around and go back.

But when the electronic voice tells me that I've arrived at my destination, I pull into the first empty spot directly across the street.

Raking a hand back through my hair, I glance at Wills for some emotional support. The kind that tells me that even though she wants to kill me for what I've done, that she's still here for me.

It's not there, though, and I don't think I'll ever see it again.

"Well?" she barks at me. "Are we going or are you just going to piss your pants right here?"

My eyes narrow dangerously at her.

I understand her hate right now but she knows what a big deal this is to me. I would have hoped that she would have given me some leeway.

"Yeah, let's go," Daphne pipes up from the back seat. "I wanna meet your dad!"

With the shake of my head, I push open the door of Willa's SUV.

I'm tired of their bickering, their constant war of wills—the need to prove that one is better or deadlier than the other.

Granted, the fact that Daphne pulled a knife on her would have normally turned me on, but trying to drive while listening to them swing their dicks at each other became boring faster than it was interesting.

That's not why I started out on this trip.

Even though Daphne was a tight little perk that I basically found on the side of the road, the more I've gotten to know her, the less about her I like, but we're finally here.

I just can't take the fucking arguing anymore,

especially since it's turned into barbs at me, so instead of waiting for them to get out of the vehicle, I decide to make my own way toward the front door of Lakyn Meyer's home by myself.

They don't deserve to meet him.

They shouldn't share in the happiness I'm hoping to feel. Even though it's marred by anger right now, I have hope that he'll change my mood.

If not instantly, then maybe after a little while.

As I tell myself to let the anger subside, his home comes into focus again.

It's nothing like I thought it would be.

For some reason, the text messages, the emails, the breathing on the other end of the line somehow painted a picture in my mind that this would be a fucking celestial palace.

Instead, I find myself almost to the door of a Spanish mission-style home, painted white on the outside to hide what I assume is one of the hugest blemishes of humanity within.

I run a hand back through my hair again to try and make myself look somewhat presentable for a man that probably cares fuck all about my existence, then raise my fist and knock on the wooden door.

I glance at the SUV over my shoulder and grit my teeth when the two babbling bitches spill out into the street and continue their shouting match. Willa has a finger in Daphne's face and the latter has her hands on her hips.

If they come to blows, they'll just have to wait until I'm done here—and if they think I'm going to jump in the middle of *that* fucking debacle, they'll be waiting for the rest of their lives.

With a grunt, I raise my fist and bang it against the door again. Perhaps I shouldn't be approaching this situation with anger in my heart, but I can't help it. The two of them seemed damned determined to make this meeting as miserable for me as possible and I'm channeling their fucking bitching into my knocking.

I have to calm down. I can't let them ruin this momentous occasion. Especially not if I was stuck in a fucking truck all this time for no goddamn reason.

"Cut it the fuck out!" I shout as I turn sideways to glare at Willa and Daphne. But they don't hear me, and if they do, then they don't care.

Just like everyone else in my life.

"Can I help you?" a voice greets me uncertainly.

I turn my attention back toward the now half-opened front door and raise an eyebrow. The green eyes I find myself looking into are tired but light up almost immediately when they lock on mine.

Almost as if they suddenly filled with... hope.

"Are you—?" the tired man stops his question short as a curious smile curves the edges of his lips. He steps out and shakes his head as he lets out a chuckle. "What am I even saying? Of course, you are. Or at the very least, I wouldn't be surprised if you were. You look almost exactly like him. Holy shit."

I arch an eyebrow at him dangerously. I'm not in the mood for this shit right now.

"Listen, is he here or not?" I snap at him. "I've been stuck in that truck for way too fucking long to stand here and let someone I don't even know ogle me."

"But you don't know Lakyn either. Not that I'm aware of anyway, because who knows where he goes when he gets into one of his moods," he replies with that curious smile still on his lips as he lets his hands drop to his sides. "I'm just surprised that you're here is all."

"So, is *he* here?" I ask again, my tone dripping with venom. I don't want to be unkind to this guy because he looks like he's had a rough enough life as it is, but I'm not going to just stand here and trade pleasantries either.

The young, frail man nods at me as his smile falters slightly. "I should probably go get him. He doesn't like surprises, though. Do you mind waiting here for a sec? I promise he'll be right out."

I look away for a moment, squaring my jaw in frustration, but what choice do I have? Besides kicking in the fucking door and going in myself, that is.

"Fine," I finally agree, testily.

He nods as he steps back into the house and closes the door behind him. I can hear his muffled voice as he shouts for Lakyn.

Deep breaths, Aftyn.

I decide to take a moment to compose myself and

maybe try to swallow some of the anger that these shrieking banshees have bestowed on me by leaning against the side of the house and doing some breathing exercises.

It never really works when I'm this angry, but it's better to try than not at all.

I watch as Willa reaches forward and shoves Daphne. Seems that good ol' Wills has had enough of trying to see her side of things and she's ready to get messy.

I wonder if she'll knife her here in public.

I tilt my head to the side as I fold a leg and place my foot against the wall. Watching them ready to assault each other is starting to calm me down, so I think I'll just stand around for a little while longer and let them go at each other's throats.

The door opens again, and the young man steps out. He glances at the scene that's moved toward the middle of the street by now, then looks at me with a raised eyebrow.

"Are they okay?" he asks me uncertainly.

"Nope."

"They shouldn't be in the middle of the—"

He stops short when another man walks out of the house and brushes by him. He's tall, well-built, and has the most impossibly shiny, messy yet neat, black hair that I've ever seen.

And he's heading straight toward Willa and Daphne.

"Is that—?"

The young man looks at me and nods instantly as the hope that was in his eyes vanishes and he begins to chew his lower lip nervously.

I push off the wall and slip my hands into my pockets as I watch the scene unfold curiously.

The man that has just been confirmed to be Lakyn Meyer walks right into the street, grabs each girl by their arms and hauls them to the other side of the road. Wills wrenches her arm out of his grip and looks like she's about ready to deck him, when her pure rage is taken over by shock.

Even from here I can see her blink rapidly a few times. She looks up at him and then cranes her neck around his form to look at me, then back again.

"I guess your friend sees it too," the young man states quietly.

I watch carefully as Willa takes a step back onto the sidewalk then pushes her hair behind her ears before she starts to talk to him.

I wish I could hear what she's saying.

Daphne's looking at him curiously as she takes a step further away, but I can see that she's being held hostage by whatever the hell he looks like alone.

"That's how he works," the young man tells me knowingly as he crosses his arms over his chest again. "There isn't a goddamn thing on this Earth that Lakyn can't get with his charm."

I don't say anything because there isn't anything *to* say.

Not anymore.

I take a deep breath as I walk by the young man and attempt to break into the trio's little heart to heart, but he catches up almost instantly and shakes his head as he puts a hand on my forearm.

"Let him come to you. Don't interrupt him. Smile and thank him for everything. Even if you don't want to."

"Who the fuck *are* you?" I finally explode at him. I didn't mean to yell at him but at this point, I apparently got some rules thrown at me that I refuse to adhere to. I'm no one's bitch and I'm not going to start now.

"Ichabod," he tells me, the smile returning slightly. "What's your name?"

"Aftyn," I reply through grit teeth.

I've never once heard of an Ichabod before, but anything that ever had to do with this side of the family tree had always been sheared down whenever I asked.

He holds a hand out toward me and I take it, initiating a quick shake, then let go.

"Are you sure you want to do this?" he asks me, glancing at Lakyn again who now has his hands in the air like he's explaining something to the banshees.

"Absolutely."

He lets out a heavy sigh, then cups his hands over

his mouth. "Lakyn! You've got company!" he shouts across the street.

Lakyn turns his body slightly enough that he's still partially directing his words to the banshees, but he can see me and this Ichabod guy.

When his eyes settle on me... when I finally see the face of the man that's haunted this entire trip in the fucking flesh for the first time... I find myself wiping away an angry, lone tear.

All this time, I thought this had been some kind of a sick joke. That someone had found a man that looked like me and taunted me to the point that I would have either changed my phone number or even gotten a new e-mail address, but I called their bluff.

I called everyone's bluff.

And as Lakyn Meyer drops his hands to his side and stares at me, I wonder if I did the right thing.

Especially when he looks at me with a little bit of shock, a whole lot of curiosity, and then a grin that takes over half his face.

It takes no more than thirty seconds before he's standing right in front of me. My fists are balled at my sides in anger, in hope, when he shakes his head and lets out a friendly laugh.

"What do we have here?"

THIRTY

A Stripper Would Have Been Better

LAKYN

"Girls, come on. If you're going to fight in the street, may as well fight inside where I can enjoy it." I turn on my charming grin, spreading my arms as they stop glaring at each other long enough to look at me. These two chicks look like they're about to tear each other the fuck apart, and that's definitely a party I want a front row seat for.

"Sounds great," the blonde one says, sneering at the other one, and I fight the urge to yank a fistful of that golden shit out just so she remembers who the hell she needs to be paying attention to right now, and it's not the little redhead wearing a smile that makes me think of those creepy dolls people used to collect.

"Sure," the redhead replies, and I clap my hands together loud enough to make them both jump and look at me again. They both smile, and I don't blame them. I'm pretty damn nice to look at, and I'm glad they recognize it.

"Perfect. Then why don't we go—"

"Lakyn! You've got company!" Ichabod shouts at me from the front yard, and I glance back over my shoulder just far enough to see what the hell is so important. There's a dark-haired kid standing next to him, wiping at his face, and I don't know why Ichabod thinks this little asshole is worth interrupting me when I've got two party favors that just delivered themselves to my goddamn doorstep.

Pausing that thought, I turn back to the girls to finish my sentence. "—inside and get comfortable before you tear each other apart. I'm just going to go handle something. Why don't you grab your shit and come on in?"

Whatever the two teenage chicks say is clearly not important enough for my brain to pay attention, but the look of adoration in their eyes is exactly what I need today. A nice little ego boost to get over Ichabod's weird fucking attitude. He's been twitchy all damn week, and I haven't even fucked him that hard or choked him out on my dick. I've been *real* fucking nice, and he's over here picking up strays off our doorstep.

Winking at the girls, I turn around and face Ichabod again, dropping my arms to my sides as I watch the kid that's staring at me like I'm the goddamn second coming. Although, something about him does seem... familiar, and as nervous as Ichabod looks, I have a feeling this is going to be a lot of fun. I grin, and it only stretches further as I head across the street and right up the walk to get a better look at this little asshole.

He's got his hands fisted so tight at his sides that if I handed him a piece of coal he'd probably pop out a fucking diamond but, nervous or not, he's not bad to look at. Nice mouth, nice body from what I can tell under the rumpled clothes, and I wonder what exactly it is about this kid that has Ichabod looking like he's about to piss himself.

Shaking my head, I start to laugh as I turn my gaze back to the kid. "What do we have here?"

Tilting my head, I look him up and down, but the kid doesn't say a thing. I figure he's just overwhelmed by the sight of me, which happens more often than you might think. I've been told it's just my aura, or my charisma, or some fucking thing like that. But, since the kid is dumbstruck, I turn my focus to Ichabod and let my grin stretch when his shoulders cave in slightly.

"Ichabod... did you get me a stripper for my birthday?" I ask with a chuckle, watching him and the kid turn red as Ichabod starts nodding.

"Yeah." He nods some more, like a fucking bobble head that got smacked hard. "Yeah, I did."

"Fan-fucking-tastic! Let's go inside then!" Turning, I see the girls coming up the sidewalk, bitching at each other like a pair of fucking cats trapped in a bag. I hear the door open behind me and Ichabod leads our first piece of entertainment inside while I wait for the second course. "Come on, you don't wanna miss the show."

They go silent to look at me again, the blonde one narrowing her eyes at me, and it's so damn tempting to pluck one out so she doesn't forget that the only reason I'm inviting them in at all is so they can look at me with awe while I get a lap dance. I don't know what's gone down between them, and I don't really care, but if they're going to start clawing and ripping each other's clothes off, they might as well entertain me with it—after the kid anyway.

Holding the door open like a real fucking gentleman, I let them walk in ahead of me, noticing the grungy clothes and dirty backpack on the redhead and the designer labels with accompanying designer purse on the blonde. That is a weird fucking pair to be running around together, but hopefully that just means the fight will be that much more fun to watch. The winner might just get to ride my dick before I slit her throat to stop the fucking bickering.

Rolling my eyes, I slam the door and follow them into the living room. Ichabod is standing a little behind the kid who's staring at me again, but I understand how impatient he is to start. I snap my fingers and point at the couch, glancing at the two girls. "Sit the fuck down and shut up so I can enjoy my striptease."

"Lakyn—" Ichabod starts, but one flash of my grin and he goes quiet.

"Don't spoil any more of my surprises," I tell him, and he knows me well enough by now to know that means he won't be spoiling any of *my* surprises for them either. Dropping into my chair, I clap my hands and turn all my attention to the kid. "Well, go on. Dance for me."

The kid looks like he's about to pop. His face is so red and his fists are shaking at his sides, and I think this might actually be anger instead of nerves—not that I care if he wants to do some kind of angry striptease. Everyone's got their kinks and fetishes, and I don't fault people for living their life and doing their own shit. I'm about to tell him to get on with it when he suddenly shouts, "You're my father!"

Sucking my teeth, I look at his face a little closer, beyond the nice lips that I was busy imagining wrapped around my cock up until about ten seconds ago. I do see some resemblance, but I can't think of how the fuck this could have happened. When the hell had I ever fucked a chick that got to walk away and produce a kid? Usually I make sure that my dick is the last thing they experience on this planet, which is a serious gift. I mean, what else would compare after that? Nothing. Putting them down is a mercy—and a lot of fun. But when...

Oh shit. Vegas.

I start laughing as I reach over for my pack of smokes and take one out with my teeth, lighting it up so I can take a drag and let the smoke billow out of my mouth as I explain. "You know, I always wondered what happened to that chick. She got away when I was sleeping. Must have been sloppy with the knots that night, but who could blame me? Long drives always take it out of me. That's why I tend to stay close to home."

Slapping the arm of the chair, I lean forward, bracing my elbows on my knees. I take another drag and look this kid over from head to toe. Nice hair, nice face, tall for his age—whatever that fucking is.

How long ago was Vegas? I think about asking Ichabod, but it doesn't matter enough.

Blowing smoke toward the kid, I grin when he just keeps glaring at me. I relax back in the chair, tapping my cigarette before I point it at him. "So, why the hell did you come here?"

"I just wanted to meet you," he says, and I wonder if he actually thinks that's a good enough reason to show up on my fucking doorstep. Not like the kid knows how amazing I am, or how much fun I could have with the two girls sitting behind him with their eyes glued on me. Worshiping me. Hell, maybe *this* could be the start of my cult following. If I let them live long enough anyway.

Although, the thought of a cult does give me another good idea, and it's been too fucking long since I checked on Satan's errant bitch. Laughing low, I jab the cigarette out beside me and turn to look at Ichabod who I'm pretty sure is still contemplating passing out on me—but he knows what happens if he does that. Facing the kid, I rub my hands together and stand up, noting that I've still got a few inches on the little accident.

"Well, kid, if we're having a fucking family reunion..." I let my grin stretch as I meet those blue eyes that look damn close to mine. "You really should meet your Aunt Beatrix."

About Yolanda Olson

Yolanda Olson is a *USA Today* bestselling and award-winning author. Born and raised in Bridgeport, CT where she currently resides, she usually spends her time watching her favorite channel, Investigation Discovery. Occasionally, she takes a break to write books and test the limits of her mind. Also an avid horror movie fan, she likes to incorporate dark elements into the majority of her books.

You can keep in touch with her on Facebook, Twitter, and Instagram.

More books by Yolanda:
Inferno: https://mybook.to/Inferno_
Death Blooms: http://mybook.to/deathblooms
Scavengers: http://mybook.to/scavengers

Sign up for Yolanda's newsletter here.

http://eepurl.com/gSvPo9

About Jennifer Bene

Jennifer Bene is a *USA Today* bestselling author of dangerously sexy and deviously dark romance. From BDSM, to Suspense, Dark Romance, and Thrillers—she writes it all. Always delivering a twisty, spine-tingling journey with the promise of a happily-ever-after.

Don't miss a release! Sign up for the newsletter to get new book alerts (and a free welcome book) at:

http://jenniferbene.com/newsletter

You can find her online throughout social media with username @jbeneauthor and on her website:

www.jenniferbene.com

Also by Jennifer Bene

The Thalia Series (Dark Romance)

Security Binds Her *(Thalia Book 1)*

Striking a Balance *(Thalia Book 2)*

Salvaged by Love *(Thalia Book 3)*

Tying the Knot *(Thalia Book 4)*

The Thalia Series: The Complete Collection

The Beth Series (Dark Romance)

Breaking Beth *(Beth Book 1)*

Fragile Ties Series (Dark Romance)

Destruction *(Fragile Ties Book 1)*

Inheritance *(Fragile Ties Book 2)*

Redemption *(Fragile Ties Book 3)*

Dangerous Games Series (Dark Mafia Romance)

Early Sins *(A Dangerous Games Prequel)*

Lethal Sin *(Dangerous Games Book 1)*

Standalone Dark Romance

Imperfect Monster

Corrupt Desires

Deviant Attraction: A Dark and Dirty Collection

Reign of Ruin

Mesmer

Jasmine

Crazy Broken Love

Standalone BDSM Ménage Romance

The Invitation

Reunited

Dark Suspense / Horror

Burned: An Inferno World Novella

Scorched: A New Beginning

Noxious *(Anathema Book 1)*

Mephitic *(Anathema Book 2)*

Viperous *(Anathema Book 3)*

Appearances in the Black Light Series (BDSM Romance)

Black Light: Exposed *(Black Light Series Book 2)*

Black Light: Valentine Roulette *(Black Light Series Book 3)*

Black Light: Roulette Redux *(Black Light Series Book 7)*

Black Light: Celebrity Roulette *(Black Light Series Book 12)*

Black Light: Charmed *(Black Light Series Book 15)*

Black Light: Roulette War *(Black Light Series Book 16)*

Black Light: The Beginning *(Black Light Series Book 17.5)*

Black Light: Unbound *(Black Light Series Book 18)*

Books Released As Cassandra Faye

Daughters of Eltera Series (Dark Fantasy Romance)

Fae *(Daughters of Eltera Book 1)*

Tara *(Daughters of Eltera Book 2)*

Standalone Paranormal Romance

Hunted *(The Dirty Heroes Collection Book 13)*

One Crazy Bite

Dangerous Magic